TEMPTATION OF THE BUTTERFLY

DYNASTY LORDS (ANNIVERSARY EDITION)

MICHELLE M. PILLOW

MICHELLE M. PILLOW® - MICHELLEPILLOW.COM

Science Fiction Romance

A princess expected to uphold honor and tradition, a man dishonored and shunned by the very society she rules. Their passion may be hot, their wills strong, but how can she fall for the man who might be trying to kill her?

When her life is threatened by mysterious events only she can see, Princess Fen has more to worry about than finding a husband. Too bad her parents don't feel the same way. Desperate to keep her from leaving the planet like her sister, they decide to play matchmaker, inviting wealthy, noble suitors to the palace.

But it's not a rich suitor who catches her eye, it's the commoner, Aaron Piers—a man who's past is clouded with dishonor, a man without family, a man she could never consider marrying. Though her desire for him burns hot, their relationship can never be. Besides, he might just be the one trying to kill her.

Seduction of the Phoenix
Temptation of the Butterfly

Dynasty Lords: Seduction of the Phoenix is part of the Qurilixen World. The Qurilixen World is an extensive collection of science fiction and futuristic romance novels by award-winning author, Michelle M. Pillow. It's hard to believe so much time has passed since the first Dragon Lords book was published (2004) and the Qurilixen World was born, and has since grown into a massive collection of books. Currently, there are 33 books and counting in 7 series installments.

If you're not familiar with the Qurilixen World series, I have a ton of information and reading lists on my website. It includes: Dragon Lords series, *Lords of the Var*® series, Space Lords series, Dynasty Lords series, Captured by a Dragon-Shifter series, Galaxy

Alien Mail Order Brides series, and more! Watch for an exciting announcement to come in 2018 (Be sure to join my newsletter!).

Browse the series at Qurilixen.com

Over the course of my career I've written in many genres—futuristic, science fiction, historical, paranormal, fantasy, dark paranormal, contemporary, and most recently cozy mystery. I've written for many publishers—big New York and London traditional publishers, e-first and now indie self-pub. I've published many series, won national awards, spoken at conferences, made bestseller lists, started the successful The Raven Books with the awesome Mandy M. Roth, and met some wonderful readers. It's been a wild ride. And I'm excited that I finally took the time to revisit these stories.

As a writer you learn so much (or at least you should), and it was a pleasure to revisit and update this series. The series name has been changed from Zhang Dynasty to Dynasty Lords, mainly to help new readers match the titles to the series. So many have emailed over the years saying they had no idea that this spin-off series was part of the Qurilixen World.

It is amazing to have readers still asking for more books in a world after over a decade. I am grateful every day for my readers. Thank you! Your emails, social media spreading of the word, and support of my work has been more than an author could ever hope for.

It's the reviews and sharing of readers like you that truly help a series maintain success.

Happy Reading!
Michelle M. Pillow

The Playful Prince
The Bound Prince
The Rogue Prince
The Pirate Prince

Captured by a Dragon-Shifter Series
Determined Prince
Rebellious Prince
Stranded with the Cajun
Hunted by the Dragon
Mischievous Prince
Headstrong Prince

Space Lords Series
His Frost Maiden
His Fire Maiden
His Metal Maiden
His Earth Maiden
His Woodland Maiden

Qurilixen Lords Series

Dragon Prince

Marked Prince

More Coming Soon!

To learn more about the Qurilixen World series of
books and to stay up to date on the latest book list
visit www.MichellePillow.com

To John

"Make her burn for me. Make her burn..."

Thin trails of smoke curled in the air, surrounding the offering of wine and bread before disappearing along the latticework above the low altar. Darkness shadowed the room, hiding the lone figure who knelt in meditative prayer, rocking back and forth in desperation as passion burned inside him, deep, haunting, all consuming.

The dark silk of his robes billowed into a glossy pool around his feet and fell past his hands to cover them completely. The material swam around him as if he were a child in his father's clothing. Like most of the men on his planet, he wore his hair long, but he wasn't like the other men, not really. He was different, a part of them but unaccepted.

The man rocked faster, his whispered pants growing with each anxious twitch of his body.

Soon. He'd see her again soon.

"Make her burn for me, as I burn for her. Make her burn for me. I beg of you, honored ancestors. Bring me her heart. Make it burn."

IMPERIAL PALACE of the Zhang Dynasty, Honorable City, Muntong Territory, Planet of Lintian

"*QING BANG-ZHU WO!*" Princess Zhang Fen yelled in terror, as she tried not to inhale the thick black smoke which filled the air of her bedchamber. Fire danced in spiraling patterns all around her. She tried to escape through her front door, which led to the hall and front foyer of the building which housed the royal living quarters. Flames cut her off, engulfing the walls as they nearly seared her skin with the intensity of the heat.

"Please, help me. Anyone," she screamed again, but it did no good. No one came to rescue her. The royal quarters was only one building out of a great many which made up the imperial palace of Honorable City. How could no one hear her calls for help? Where were her brothers who shared the building with her? Had the fire already consumed them?

A chill racked her spine, causing a brief shiver amidst the fiery temperature. The ghostly presence of her ancestors surrounded her, for who else could it be? Ancestors showed themselves to those they wished to guide, and she was in desperate need. Fen looked for their transparent forms, hoping they were there to lead her out of harm's way. She couldn't see them through the smoke.

"Grandmother? Are you here?" she whispered, knowing her great-grandmother, Zhang An, would show herself if she was. Since her death, An had been residing in the Sacred Chamber hidden within the walls of the Hall of Infinite Wisdom.

Fen was in good standing with the ancestors. She always left offerings, especially for An, who loved wine. Ever since Fen's mother, the empress, had stopped leaving the drink for the old spirit, Fen had sneaked wine into the Sacred Chamber.

The empress was upset with An because the spirit hadn't been forthcoming when she'd predicted Princess Mei's future. Everyone thought Fen's sister would marry Prince Song Lok, whose family ruled the only other dynasty on the planet of Lintian. Instead, Mei had wed a space captain and was flying around the high skies, far away from her palace home. She'd just given birth to a son, the first royal grandchild. The empress missed her youngest daughter dearly and resented not having an active hand in raising the boy.

"Grandmother An, if you get me out of this, I promise to leave you twice as much wine tonight." Fen watched the smoke for any sign that she was heard. Still there was no answer. Out of all her ancestors, An meddled in their lives the most.

Then, where was she? What better time to *meddle?*

Right now, Fen would take the help of any of the spirits who resided within the palace. They could be anywhere at any time, but usually avoided private areas like bedrooms.

Another chill washed over her and she knew a spirit was close, but she couldn't see who. Why weren't they helping her escape? Or was there no escaping these flames? Were they waiting for her to join them in death?

"I'm not ready. I'm not ready," Fen said, tears welling in her eyes. Part of her clung to the hope of liberation, believed so fully she'd be saved that she didn't consider the possibility of getting hurt. But, as no one came and the flames grew, she wasn't as confident. "*Qing*, please, I'm not ready. I'm not ready to die!"

The dark silk on her bed melted and curled with the heat, matching the melting silk tapestries that burned along her walls. Her gaze flew to the thin doorways separating the chambers of her room. Both doors had burned, revealing the rooms beyond. Her living space and her decontaminator room were also on fire.

"Grandfather Manchu?" she asked, hoping to appeal to Zhang An's son. The two were often at odds, but if one wasn't going to help her then maybe the other spirit would. The building housed the private quarters of the royal siblings, and she prayed her brothers had gotten out safely and would find a way to rescue her. "I beg you, Manchu, help me. Protect me. Protect my family."

Wood crackled as she once more tried to reach the thick bedroom door which would lead to the outside hall and to safety. A piece of the door fell away and she saw the hall on the other side. It looked fresh and clean, unlike her bedroom. Smoke charred the gold inlay on the carved wood, and she was forced to her knees as it became harder to breathe. The tears in her eyes dried before they could trail down her hot cheeks, as all moisture was sapped from the air.

A large beam fell from the ceiling and she screamed, scrambling back to curl into a ball. There was nowhere to go.

"*Qing*, help!" Fen closed her eyes tight, trying to gain the courage to push through the flames toward safety. "*Qing,* I don't want to die like this."

"Princess?"

A shout followed by the crash of her door sounded over her, propelling her into action. Finally, she was saved. Before opening her eyes, she stood. "I'm here—"

Fen froze, her voice dying in her throat as the heat instantly left her skin. The flames were gone and the room stood exactly as it had before the fire started—from the wrinkled covers on her bed where she'd been sleeping, to the delicate butterfly and peony patterns on her rugs.

She coughed, a small puff of smoke leaving her lips, the only evidence as to what had happened moments before. She panted for breath, still choked from the heat as she looked around in shock. Embroidered blue silk again hung over her walls and lay across her bed. The thin doors were shut, completely unharmed as they hid the living area and decontaminator from view.

Shaking, she looked at the main door in confusion. Its gold inlay shone like it had before she went to bed, the thick wood unmarred.

Dark blue eyes, the shade of her favorite color, met hers over the short distance. They belonged to the man waiting in the entryway, his body tense as if ready for battle.

"Princess?" the man repeated, his deep tone softer this time. The rich, low sound of his voice rolled over her like cooling water to her heated skin.

Fen was too stunned to answer. A new fire sprang to life inside her stomach, curling with a gentle warmth. What had happened to the flames in her bedchamber? What magic did this man have that could stop fire and make it as if it had never happened?

Her limbs went numb as she looked at his handsome face. A rush of gratitude came over her, even though there was no longer any fire to be rescued from. Part of her wanted to run to him, throw her arms around him in thanks for stopping the flames, to sprinkle grateful kisses on his cheeks and bless him for what he'd done. But there was more than gratitude that hit her when she looked at him. It was an improper feeling, a feeling of attraction and interest, a curling of awareness that here stood a man, alone with her in her bedchambers where no others were allowed. The rule was not one of the palace, but her own. Men only brought complication, and she did not wish to be gossiped about by the palace servants.

"If you have no need of my services, Princess, please excuse me." The man bowed politely and moved to pull the door shut.

She gaped, wide-eyed at him, not wanting him to go but not knowing what to say to make him stay.

"*Duibuqi*. Excuse me, Princess, I did not mean to intrude—"

"Wait," Fen demanded just before the door shut completely, finally compelled to speak.

The man stopped, and he opened the door once more, standing at rigid attention. His eyes did not meet hers again, and she finally felt as if she could breathe in his presence. She studied him, feeling a pull toward him. Had she seen him somewhere before? Did she know him? He wasn't dressed as a palace guard, nor was he dressed as a noble. The plain black of his clothing was oddly devoid of any decoration, though it was spun from silk and had the traditional Mandarin collar and frog buttons.

Fen continued to study him, her mind wrapping completely around the mystery. His brown hair was long, pulled into a traditional topknot. Though there was a hint of Lintianese in his strong features, his cheekbones were too prominent, and his lips curved in such a way as to make them unfamiliar.

Whoever this man was, she'd guess he was only half-Lintianese by birth. His pronunciation of the language was flawless, indicating he'd been raised in their ways or had access to a stellar language upload program.

He was taller than most men Fen had been around, though not so tall as Mei's space captain husband who practically towered over her. Captain Jarek of the Var also happened to be a foreign cat-shifting prince.

"Who are you?" she asked the handsome stranger, not moving.

"Aaron," he answered. His gaze focused on her feet. Fen resisted the urge to hide her toes from view. They tingled with just a stare from him.

"Aaron?" she repeated, rolling the foreign name around in her mouth. "What is your family name? Or is that your family name?"

"Piers." The answer was clipped.

"How did you get in here, Piers Aaron?" Fen asked.

"Forgive my intrusion, Princess, I heard you scream for help as I walked by and thought you needed rescuing." His hands gripped in light fists at his side. They were strong, calloused hands, the hands of a worker. He glanced around the room, refusing to look directly at her. "I see now you were merely playacting. Forgive my mistake. *Duibuqi*, excuse me."

Fen tensed. There was something in his tone that bothered her. It took her a moment to realize it was disdain, mixed with a touch of pity. He thought she was crazy, screaming for help when there was nothing to be rescued from. So much for the theory that this man had magic. Could she really blame his reproach? All evidence of her dire situation had disappeared, making it appear as if she'd been screaming like a madwoman for no reason. Fen hardly needed rescuing from her bedclothes.

The man was so serious, so rigid as he waited for her to dismiss him, that she couldn't help but tease him in the hopes of putting him at ease. "Do you know there is a penalty for wandering about outside the royal chambers, even if you were waiting to save me from myself?"

Aaron glanced up at her words, and she tried to smile to show she was joking, but the look in his dark eyes stopped her cold. What she could only describe as resentment burned within his gaze.

Out of all the Zhang children, Fen was most gifted with charm. It was more than the natural ability to put people at ease, it was a power bestowed upon her at birth by their sacred Jade Phoenix. When she spoke, she could induce a person to tell the truth or to show their true emotions. And, to an extent, she could control them by playing their emotions against them with the power of persuasion. It was a great responsibility, one Fen never used for ill intent.

Her powers being as they were, she knew she shouldn't have been surprised to see the raw emotion in the man's eyes. To anyone else, he would appear stoic and calm, but she saw his resentment, his borderline anger and hate that bubbled just beneath the surface. Did he hate her? Resent her? Her family? The palace? It was hard to say without knowing who he was or why he was within the walls of Honorable City.

The sudden impact of his hidden emotions made her uneasy.

"I have the emperor's permission to stay in Péng

You Hall." Aaron lifted his jaw, the gesture one of pride. Then, as if catching himself, he deliberately lowered his eyes once more. Pride was not something she saw too often in commoners, at least not when they knew she was there.

"You're a guest?" she asked in surprise.

Aaron nodded once. Fen wasn't sure if she should believe him. Maybe he trespassed on palace grounds. A thief? Instantly she dismissed the thought. A thief wouldn't have stopped to save her. But, then who? Being one of the four unmarried royal children still residing at the palace, she was expected to welcome any of their guests. Although, at fifty-one years of age, she hardly considered herself a child, even if she did look exactly as she had thirty years ago.

"Here?" she persisted. "You're a guest here in the palace?"

He said again, "I have the emperor's permission to stay in Péng You Hall."

Fen nodded weakly, completely aware that she sounded like an imbecile as she forced her poor rescuer to repeat himself as if she were a child. It was hard to gather her thoughts so soon after the strange fire. The pull of his nearness wasn't helping her concentrate—though to look at him, the pull was entirely one-sided.

"If you have no need of me, Princess, I'll take my leave of you." Aaron glanced up, again showing her the dark blue of his gaze. Fen gestured at him in dismissal. He pulled the door shut behind him and left without further comment.

For a long, silent moment, she stared after him, looking at the gold inlay on the door without really seeing it.

Suddenly, as she remembered the fire that had awakened her from her dreams, she sprang into action. Fen grabbed her robe off a nearby chair. As she ran, she slipped it over her shoulders, hurrying to make sure none of her siblings was harmed by the strange disappearing inferno.

The flames hadn't been a dream. They couldn't have been. They had felt so real.

A vision? she wondered, confused. *An omen or warning?*

Foresight was Shen's gift from the Jade Phoenix, not hers.

In total, there were six royal siblings. Prince Haun was the oldest and heir to the throne. He had strength and a warrior's heart. When the time came, he would make a great emperor. Second oldest was

Jin, with the gift of knowing and understanding the past. Then Lian, who was blessed with grace, both in movement and temperament, and with knowledge of the present. He could defuse any situation with logic and made one fine dancer. Fen was next in line, born a few years before her younger brother, Shen. And the baby of the family was Mei, whose soul was like the wind, blowing free. Mei was pure instinct, led by the elements who whispered their secrets in her ear.

Beyond that, there were two siblings-by-marriage —Mei's husband, Jarek, and Jin's wife. Jin had married a foreign woman, Francesca La Rosa. They were living quite happily in the countryside away from the palace, where they were completing the building for a school to teach martial arts.

Since both siblings had found happiness in foreign arms, why shouldn't Fen too be attracted to a man who wasn't wholly of Lintianese birth? It wasn't like she was going to marry Piers Aaron, she was just a little bit interested in him on a romantic level. Okay, a fair bit interested in him—naturally assuming he was a guest at the palace, like he said. She wondered if the emperor and empress would see it that way. In the immediate family, it was no secret her mother was disappointed in the matches Jin and Mei had made.

An ache filled her as she thought of her sister. She missed Mei. It was hard being around men all the time. She had hoped Francesca would be more open to friendship, but the woman was still too guarded. If only Fen had someone to talk to who wasn't a brother.

She thought of her strange rescuer. Who was he really? What was he doing in the palace?

Stopping at Haun's door, she pounded her hand against it. "Haun? It's me, Fen. Haun? Are you safe?"

A sleepy-eyed Haun opened the door, mid-yawn. Irritated, he grumbled, "*Hao le, hao le*, that's enough. Stop pounding, Fen, I hear you. What are you yelling about?"

He held the door to hide his waist, letting her see his naked chest. Fen averted her eyes briefly, as it was apparent her brother wasn't dressed for the day.

"You're not on fire?" Fen asked, again looking up at her brother.

"What?" He blinked in confusion, shaking his head in denial of the obvious question.

"No?" Turning before he could speak, she hurried toward Lian's door, telling Haun, "Okay, good, I'm glad."

Fen stopped to pound on Lian's door. He too answered with a yawn.

"What's happening?" Lian asked, more alert than Haun had been.

"I had a vision or something," Fen said. "You're unharmed?"

Lian nodded in the affirmative. "*Shi.*"

"No fire?"

"No." Lian frowned.

"Ah, good," Fen answered, turning to check on Shen.

"Wait, Fen," Haun emerged from his room to follow her. He had put clothes on. "What's going on?"

"She said she had a vision," Lian answered for her.

"A vision?" Haun gasped. "But, Fen, you don't have visions."

"I know that." Fen didn't have a chance to knock as Shen slid open the door. "Any fire in there?"

"Fire? No." Shen's eyes were clear, signifying he'd been awake for a while.

"Good, you're all safe. It's just me." Fen sighed with relief. To Shen, she asked, "Can I come in?"

Shen stepped back, waving his hand to gesture her in. Fen walked past him. The aqua color of the silk décor, embroidered with the ancient symbol of a fish amongst waves, reminded her of being underwater.

"This is going to be interesting," Lian said behind her. She heard her brothers entering the room but was unsure where to begin the explanation of what had happened. A fire, but no proof of fire. How was she going to explain that?

"Now, *jie jie,*" Haun said. "Talk to us. What's this about a vision and fire?"

Fen nodded, going on to tell them about her bizarre morning.

2

THE SUN SHONE down over the beautiful imperial palace grounds, giving warmth to the early morning. Aaron took a deep, cleansing breath as he stood on the path outside the royal bedchambers. The air was sweet and clean, but that wasn't unusual for the planet. Lintian was blessed with fair weather and a lush countryside—not that anyone could see the countryside from within the palace. A long wall guarded Honorable City, protecting it from the outside world. The city consisted of the palace buildings and surrounding grounds. On the outside, the walls were protected by a wide moat to keep commoners out.

Growing up outside the palace walls as a boy, Aaron had stared at Honorable City, awed by the people who lived hidden away from the rest of the galaxy. Like other Lintianese children who were not born into privilege, he used to fantasize what it would be like to be an emperor or, in the very least, a nobleman—to be rich and powerful, to have servants and means.

The palace was beautiful, but as an adult, he couldn't see himself living inside its walls his entire life. Not that he wished to live where he did now. His village of *Haohe* was like every other Lintianese village he'd seen. Short, thatched-roof farmhouses were clustered together forming a tightly knit community where everyone knew everyone's business. Though no one spoke of his past, they knew.

Lady Hsin, his employer, owned the village. The people worked in her factories, warehouse, and fields. Aaron was one of the highest-ranking workers, but nothing could take away the dishonor that marred him. If he stayed in the village, it was likely he'd never marry, never have a family or a real home. Sure, women took their pleasure with him—most in secret—for he worked hard to assure he was a good lover. He often liked to escape to the nearby hills, with their sea of yellow-blue grasses that surrounded the most beautiful creek on the planet.

He understood things better now that he was

older, compared to when he was an awestruck young boy running around barefoot and peeking in at noble families in trepidation. Money and power did not make honor, they merely demanded it. Both could be lost within a blink of the eye. Whole worlds could end in mere seconds. Aaron knew. His whole world had ended in such a way. And his honor had been ripped from him with just a few short sentences.

Aaron had come to the imperial palace determined not to like what he saw. It was hard, considering the buildings and grounds really were beautiful. But what use did he have for these gilded treasures? Men like him didn't belong in palaces. Men like him didn't belong on this planet.

He would have left, had thought of it often, but something always kept him from going. At first, it was because he needed money to get off the planet. Lady Hsin gave him a job. Then, he thought to be in love. She was a farmer's daughter from a nearby village. He met her in the forest near *Haohe*. But when she found out who he was, she'd stopped talking to him, going so far as to deny knowing him in public. Now he knew it wasn't love, but lust that had driven his emotions.

He'd thrown himself into work and before he knew it, he'd climbed his way up to the top until he was in charge of much of the property, and the days just kept slipping by until he found himself here, in the palace, doing a job for the imperial family.

Aaron looked at his hands. They were rough, calloused from working in the mulberry fields and in the factory. A thin scar led up his forearm from his palm. He tried to remember where he'd gotten it but couldn't. The old injury was just one of the great many that littered his body.

"What am I doing here?" he whispered, balling his hand into a fist. As much as he understood his place, he wanted more. That was why he was here. He was here to make more for himself, to elevate his station.

The city was a fortress, laid out over three quarters of a mile by a half mile of land. In the center was the largest structure, the Hall of Infinite Wisdom, set high upon stone to tower over the surrounding courtyard and gardens. Its roof could be seen from many points along the pathways. Also within the compound were practice halls where the royal family and imperial guards could exercise. There was a building where they paid homage to their ancestors, a library, an archery range, as well as the Exalted Hall used for weddings and private ceremonies. Barracks for the guards were near the weapons chamber, which wasn't far from where Aaron was standing.

Delicate flowers bloomed throughout the courtyard and along the walking paths. Pink buds intermingled with dark blue, eight-pointed stars with golden centers. Eight was a number of fortune, and the flowers were planted to bring luck to the palace and those within. Though, ironically, the blue *meili fa* flowers attracted *qizajian*. The tiny butterflies had small bodies with large black wings, which formed the Old Earth number seven when they flapped forward in flight. Seven represented death.

The pretty pink flowers made him think of another butterfly, one hidden behind the walls of the royal chambers.

Princess Zhang Fen. All the beauty of the imperial palace paled with the thought of her. It had been so long since he'd seen her, but until that morning she'd never laid her eyes on him. She was a princess and he was little more than a servant. Why would she see him within a crowd of many? Why would she know who he was? Her name had been whispered and blessed since her birth.

One of his earliest memories on Lintian was his foreigner's name being spat at him like a curse by a grandmother who wasn't pleased to see the orphan boy on her doorstep in need of care. *Yang gui zi*, she had called him, *foreign devil*. His mother had treated him like a prince, and when his parents died, he'd lost everything, even the pretend title.

Princess Fen was the type of lady common men stared at. She was a dream, a fantasy, and she was renowned for her meek and gentle manners, which were second only to her beauty. Her hair gleamed, the long dark locks rich in color, matching her magnetic eyes. Slender and graceful, her willowy form seemed to float above the ground as she moved. Though she'd merely stood before him that morning, he remembered her walk well. When she came through his village, he would stare at her, watching her, foolishly wishing she'd look his way and notice him.

It had been years since he'd last seen her, and he never would have approached her now without cause.

Aaron was sweaty from his morning exercise. He'd awakened before dawn out of habit and had been about to go bathe when he'd heard the princess' cry. The old clothes were hardly how he wished to greet her for the first time, and he was determined to make a better impression when next they met. He had no clue what had frightened her, only that she'd been huddled on the floor, screaming at the top of her lungs for help.

Had she gone mad? No one else came to save her. Were the princes and palace guards accustomed to her loud shouts?

"Forget about her," he whispered. Forcing himself to walk toward the Péng You Hall, he tried to put the princess from his mind. "Women like her don't know men like me."

3

"Xiaoxin, Fen, you're about to wear a hole in my floor." Shen chuckled, uncrossing his ankles as he continued to lounge back on his bed. He shifted lazily, as if trying to get comfortable while watching his sister pace the bedchamber. He was the most contemplative of them and often spoke with a sound mind. "What I don't get is, are you upset that Aaron is really a guest, or that you had a nightmare about fire?"

Haun had informed them that the mysterious Aaron was truly a guest, but not one worthy of informing Fen about. Apparently, the man worked for Lady Hsin in the village near the noblewoman's home. Fen knew the lady well and had visited her home often over the years. Lady Hsin's family had produced the finest silks on the planet since her people had first migrated to Lintian from Old Earth, and they were the sole supplier to the imperial family.

"Why is he here, anyway?" Fen asked, trying to shove the memory of him from her mind. His blue eyes haunted her with their intensity. If he was here on business, why was he so upset? "We usually make the trip to Lady Hsin's for new clothes. I like it that way. It's one of the only times I get out of the palace."

"The empress has ordered new silk tapestries from Lady Hsin to redecorate the guest chambers and some of the palace halls. He's here to help with the order, taking measurements, whatever it is they do," Haun said. "I had some of his helpers fit me for new tunics. I figured I might as well while they were here."

"Sister, are you sure the fire you felt wasn't something else?" Lian asked, standing near the door. He looked as if he was trying to be delicate, but she saw the hidden smile in his eyes. Haun was behind him, leaning against the wall, his arms crossed over his chest. All brothers had the same semi-amused look.

"The fire was real," Fen answered. So what if it had been many, many, *many* years since she'd taken a lover.

"Mm-hmm," Shen said. "Are you sure it wasn't just a bad dream?"

Like all her brothers, Shen was handsome and refined. She loved him dearly.

"Or a very good dream?" Haun teased, lifting his brows mischievously. Fen loved it when he became playful. Often he was so serious, burdened with responsibility.

"The fire was real," she repeated. "It had nothing to do with—"

"So you admit that you found him to be fire-worthy?" Shen asked.

"I admit nothing." Fen tried to sound stern.

"Then possibly it was just a nightmare, Fen. It would make more sense than a vision," Shen said.

Right now, she didn't want to be told she was imagining things. The fire had been real. She'd experienced the heat on her skin. She'd smelled the smoke. The fear she'd felt was real. "It wasn't a dream."

"I've had dreams that felt real as I was having them," Lian said.

"I've had those too, but this didn't feel like that." Fen frowned. Maybe she was crazy. There was no proof of what she claimed.

"Then what was it?" Haun asked.

"I'm not sure, but I was awake, and it was as real as this bed or the rug. Do you think it's a bad omen? Am I to die by fire?" Fen shook in trepidation. After saying the words aloud, she stopped pacing and looked at Shen. Once she'd had time to think of the morning's events, she'd grown fearful. Waking up to a flaming bedchamber couldn't be a good thing.

Shen closed his eyes. "Not anytime soon, I don't see."

Fen relaxed. She'd come to Shen with this because of his power of foresight. A deep thinker, Shen well understood the paths people walked. He might not know why, but he could see where they would end up due to their actions. If he didn't see death by flames for her, then the odds were good she wasn't going to die in a fire. But, then what did the flames mean?

"Hmm, curious," Shen said under his breath. His eyes were still closed.

"What?" Fen demanded. "What is curious?"

He looked at her in mischief.

"Shen." She rushed for his bed, placing her hands on the end by his feet. "What did you see? Tell me."

"A wedding," he answered, grinning.

"A wedding?" Fen's stomach tensed. "What do you mean a wedding? Whose wedding?"

His grin widened. She heard the other two chuckling behind her.

"No." Fen shook her head. "*Bu shi.* No."

"Fen—" Haun began.

"*Hao le.*" Fen crossed her arms before her, lifting her chin slightly. "How can you say something like that, Shen? What right have you to predict anything with such certainty? You know your powers aren't that strong. A proper wedding takes time to plan and, well, the further ahead you see, the more indistinguishable it becomes and...you just have no right to say that to me."

"The emperor told me," Shen answered calmly.

"What? Our father told you as much?" Fen blinked several times, turning to look at the other two for confirmation. Both Haun and Lian nodded. "Has he arranged something? He has picked a husband for me?"

"No," Shen sat up, looking impossible in his merriment.

"Then what are you talking about?" she demanded, not liking this game they were making of teasing her.

"He's arranged for you to meet with potential

noblemen," Lian snorted, unable to hold back his laugh as he told her. "You're to be courted."

"What?" Fen couldn't believe what she was hearing. "Why would he...?"

"Mother's afraid you'll marry a man who isn't..." Haun paused, looking almost embarrassed.

"Isn't...?" she prompted.

"From here," Shen finished, trying to be delicate.

"She's afraid I'll marry a foreigner like Mei and Jin, isn't she?" Fen shook her head. "She was trying to pry the other day as to what I thought about such relationships, but I didn't think she was seriously thinking about taking matters into her own hands."

"You know the empress," Haun said, by way of telling her she should have guessed their mother would resort to such measures.

"I knew she was upset about Mei having her baby in space, but this?" Fen sighed. "Why me? Why don't one of you get married and have babies?"

Haun's expression fell slightly.

"Not you," Fen said. "I know you can't, but," she pointed at Lian and Shen, "you two can take a wife."

"Hey, we have to attend the *Qi-zi* ceremony every year," Lian said by way of defense. "We see plenty of brides."

"Oh, yeah," Fen answered dryly. "You see them

as they are led through in a line being announced. I have to entertain being courted. There is a huge difference between potential brides in a receiving line and having to put up with suitors."

All three brothers laughed, not even pretending to feel sorry for her.

"If I refuse, will it be forced?" Fen asked. Their expressions fell. "Mother thinks by having Father force my hand, I'll be compelled to marry a local."

Fen took a deep breath and held it. She wasn't sure if she was mad or annoyed, but she definitely wasn't pleased.

"A local nobleman," Shen corrected. "She's got her heart set on it, something about not wanting to risk losing you."

"Wonderful." Fen groaned. "Mei marries and floats around space and I'm punished for it."

"Marriages are not punishment," Lian said, smirking.

"Ugh." She snarled at him. They were having too much fun at her expense.

"The empress is playing the odds. She thinks the more nobles you're forced to spend time with, the more likely you'll be to choose one," Haun said.

Fen sighed. "I'll just have to figure out a way to say no without upsetting her."

"You can't refuse," Haun said. "The empress wills it."

"What do you mean I can't? I won't be obvious about it, but surely I can charm my way out of this mess." Fen smiled, feeling a little better at the idea. "I can state my case and convince Father to change his mind."

"They've already invited the noblemen," Shen laughed.

"They arrive in a few days," Lian added.

"Why do you think our empress mother ordered the new silk be brought here to the palace for us to look at? Or did we forget to mention your new gowns?" Haun grinned. "She wants you to make a good impression."

"*WODE TIAN*. This whole idea is ridiculous," Zhang An said, floating above her great-granddaughter's head.

Fen tried to ignore the woman, but it was hard when she kept talking so loud, pacing through the air in irritation. Since no one else could see or hear the spirit, Fen didn't want to let on that An was there. To do so would only upset her mother. The empress and the old spirit were still not on speaking terms, and when they did speak it was only to argue. Fen may not appreciate the reason the men surrounding the large dinner table were in her home, but she still had pride in her family and her position as princess. It wasn't the fault of the suitors that the empress wanted her to get married, and she couldn't blame the men for accepting an invitation to the palace. Though, she would've appreciated them more if they ignored her. Instead, she was showered with compliments and gifts.

She sat on a cushion on the floor, next to a low, round dining table. Her parents were seated across from her, next to them were her brothers, and around the table on each side sat her suitors. The table was much larger than where the Zhang family normally sat, and being spread so far made conversation with the opposite side harder. Fen was glad, since she didn't want her mother hearing anything she had to say to the men. She wouldn't be outright rude, but she'd find a way to put them off.

Normally, it would have been her duty to help see to the drinks, but since there were so many, servants tended to it as they brought the food out on her mother's favorite dining set. The serving dishes and plates had big blue swirls on the white backgrounds. Like everything in the palace, they were the finest.

"I would have told you if you were to be married," An continued in her tirade. "Really. Who knows more about what the fates want? Me or her? I'm the one who's dead. I'm the one who had the gift to see—*not her.*"

Fen glanced up at her, trying to hide the gesture behind her goblet of *pu tao jiu.* The spirit was dressed in the old-fashioned style from the time of her life, except for her dark locks streaked with white. Instead of pulled up into a respectful bun, they flowed around her shoulders. The long silk sleeves of her gown drifted at her sides, silently fluttering through air. Her figure was transparent, blurring slightly with each subtle movement.

An glared at the empress, floating down to lean her mouth close to Fen's ear. "Your mother has never had foresight. I don't know what made her think she could arrange this on her own. Look at that *chunren.* I forbid you from marrying him and allowing his bloodline into the family. If you do, you'll have children as foolish as their father."

Fen followed her great-grandmother's gesture as the old woman pointed at Lord He, who was seated on the other side of the table next to Emperor Zhang. The nobleman's mouth worked in short, fast bites.

That won't be a problem, Fen thought, trying not to laugh. *And you're just mad you didn't think of this first. I know you'd like to see me wed, Grandmother. How many times have you wished for babies once more at the palace, so that some of the ancestors' souls could be reborn?*

"You've said it yourself, you don't see every-thing," Fen said under her breath, as she set down the goblet. She wished the wine was stronger. A stiff drink would have been very welcome.

"Princess?" Lord Ye Wen inquired at her side, drawing her from her thoughts.

Fen looked at him and flashed an innocent smile. Lord Ye was many years older than she was and had arrived at the palace with two of his sons, the younger, Ye Yuan, and his heir, Ye Shing. Lord Ye was a *mingong,* one of the highest ranking of nobles, and she wasn't sure if he was at the palace on behalf of himself or for his sons. By the way each of them kept eyeing her, she was sure they'd welcome her choosing any from their family line. Yuan was quiet and brooding, but she'd seen the small sparkle of hope in his eyes as they were introduced. Shing was boastful and an incorrigible flirt. He laughed a lot and had a smile that was contagious. It was clear that he was used to being in the spotlight.

When Lord Ye didn't speak, she said, "I'm told your land is very beautiful, *mingong,* and your home even more so."

Taking her words as a cue, Lord Ye began telling her of his home, describing it in great detail, from the fields of *hong jio ju* crops to the way his main dwelling sat high over his village near the *Guoh Yuan Hsi Yang* Forest, overlooking the many farmers who worked his land. Halfway through, she was sure she could vividly picture every crack in every brick in every wall. The only good thing to come out of his verbal dissertation was that the conversation didn't require much interaction on her part. It gave her time to study the other suitors.

Fen had to give her mother credit. She'd invited a wide variety of looks and personalities for her daughter to choose from. It would seem the empress was not taking chances that her plan would fail. Fen had already overheard that more nobles were to come if none of these caught her eye.

Next to Lord Ye and his sons was Tan Ho. He was the son of a noble who lived far north near the mighty Satlyun River. The Satlyun flowed north to south circumnavigating the planet, and essentially splitting the land in two. The directional flow of the water was determined by its relation to the palaces, so even with it technically flowed in the opposite direction on the other side of the globe, no one described it in such a way. The palaces were the epicenter from which all things were mapped. It separated the Zhang family's territory of Muntong in the east and the Song's territory, Singhai, in the west.

Thinking of the Song Dynasty, Fen glanced to the two men who had come to her from across the great river. The two empires weren't at war, but relations had been strained ever since the drug, *chandoo*, had been discovered in Singhai's Lin Yao Mines. Haun had been negotiating with Emperor Song to get permission to check the mines, but the emperor had yet to grant him entry. That hadn't stopped Haun from sneaking in on his own to poke around, but he couldn't say what he'd found until the emperor officially allowed him to look. They knew the drug was there, they knew it was somehow being smuggled over the Satlyun, but until the Songs allowed them to know, nothing official could be done.

Because of the delicate political state of the planet, two of the higher-ranking Singhai noblemen had been invited to the palace. The handsome yet arrogant Lord Gao, and his ancient sidekick, Lord He, who had a big hand in trade between the two empires. The Song controlled the jade mines, the main source of intergalactic trade on the planet, which helped the entire race to thrive, and the Zhang controlled elements that blessed the planet with protection from the outside world. The Zhang also had the most fertile soil, which made for agricultural goods to trade for purple jade.

Fen knew that choosing either one of them would make a good political alliance, though she hardly thought they'd make a sound marriage alliance. Both Singhai men kept to themselves, hardly speaking to her. Society and culture was different in Singhai. They were much stricter as to a woman's place. She didn't care how handsome Lord Gao was or how charming he might turn out to be, she was not going to choose him and live on the other side of the planet as his subservient bride. Political relations between them weren't *that* bad.

Six other suitors sat at the table, all sons or nephews of noblemen, most set to inherit the title themselves. Deng Li was a gentleman from the village of Changshangu. Ruan Ping's family came from the far south and Fei Bin, Chu Dun, Mou Tian, and Chi Tan all hailed from various villages west of the Zhang palace. Since the palace was the center of the territory, maps of the planet were judged from its location. So Muntong territory was considered the east, even if one was to travel straight east to the other side of the planet to technically be on the west side of the Satlyun river.

"This one looks like he was dragged under a cart at birth," An said, floating behind Fei Bin's head. The man was a little gawky but had been kind to her. Fen tried not to listen. The spirit floated behind Chu Dun. "And this one drinks too much. He's sneaked five cups of wine when he thought no one was looking. And this one, what did you call him? Mou Tian?"

Fen lifted her goblet to drink.

"I caught him pleasuring himself before dinner," An declared. "Though I must say, he was rather well endowed. If you take any of them, Fen, I vote for him."

Fen wasn't expecting her great-grandmother's comment and coughed, spewing liquor over Lord Ye's plate. The noble jumped back in surprise.

Fen covered her mouth, mortified by what she'd done.

"What?" An asked. Fen glanced at her amused great-grandmother's pale face. Why had An been in the guest chambers? The spirit knew she was supposed to give everyone privacy. Though, somehow, it wasn't surprising. She shivered, knowing she'd be paranoid when she went to get undressed that night.

Fen blinked, drawing her thoughts back to the table. Little dots of liquid spotted the table before her from where she'd spit, and everyone was looking at her in expectation.

Not knowing how else to handle the embarrassing situation, she did the only thing a princess could in such a circumstance. She pretended like her behavior was normal and looked at her suitors as if they were the silly ones for even daring to give her questioning looks. "Pl—"

"Ah, now that is a real man," An broke in once more, making it hard for Fen to concentrate. "I changed my mind, Fen. You should take that one. There is a man who will bring strong stock back to the Zhang line. Just looking at him is enough to make fresh blood rush through my ghostly veins."

"Who?" Fen asked automatically. Her eyes traveled to where her great-grandmother indicated.

Aaron.

Her breath caught in her throat to see the man from her bedchamber from a few days before. He was fully dressed in dark brown, his tunic sashed with a thick white strip around his waist. Instantly, her heart quickened and she took a deep breath. He was with one of the palace servants. She wasn't sure what they were doing, but they both studied the wall.

She'd seen him a few times in the last couple of days, and she was sure he saw her, but he never approached, and she was never given an excuse to stop him. But, when he looked at her, his dark eyes glancing ever briefly in her direction, she felt it all the way to her toes.

For the first time in a long time, she wanted to take a lover. Aaron was on the same level as a servant. She shouldn't even be thinking about him.

Fen had never been with a common man before, often forced to choose from the higher ranks due to her place in society. What would it be like to have a healthy, strong working man in her bed? Aaron was so virile, so handsome. It made her body ache just thinking of it.

Such things shouldn't be done, not even considered. The forbidden only added to her desire for him. Or maybe it was being faced with the prospect of marriage. Maybe that is why she desperately wanted to seduce the man to her bed, because he wasn't an option when it came to picking a husband.

"Princess?" Lord Ye asked, his voice strained. Fen drew her gaze back to the noble, doing her best to calm the lust in her veins. Lord Ye was a stark contrast to Aaron. Her suitors were gentlemen, raised in wealth and power. Aaron was strangely vibrant in comparison.

Empress Zhang frowned, her eyes narrowing in severe displeasure. Fen hadn't seen her mother that upset since she was a child and had used the empress' face powder as pretend magic dust over the royal garden.

"Who," Fen repeated carefully, adding, "would like to escort me on a walk through the gardens?"

"Please—" the younger Ye Yaun began, only to be cut off by his older brother.

"Allow me," said Ye Shing, standing gracefully. "It would be my honor, Princess."

Yaun frowned and turned his face toward his plate to continue brooding. Lord Ye grinned at the other suitors in victory as Shing walked around the table to help Fen up. Since her mother had insisted on the new bright pink gown with large embroidered butterflies, which cinched tightly around her waist, it was hard for Fen to get up on her own.

Nodding in gratitude, she allowed Shing to lead her from the hall. Out of all the men who could have taken her up on the offer, Shing was one of the better choices for company. In a distant way, he reminded her of her brothers—proud, handsome, strong—but there was also a smarminess to him that her brothers didn't have. She was too tired to read into him too much. It was possible that she'd only be too hard on him because of who he was and why he was in her home.

They passed near Aaron. The man stopped what

he was doing to look at her, and the potent force of the desire she carried for him stirred within her blood. She wished he was the one taking her to the gardens. The palace servant next to him instantly bowed. Aaron was slower to follow. His eyes met hers boldly, holding them for a brief, sizzling second before turning toward the floor.

"Princess, are you ready?" Shing prompted. She turned to him, forcing a smile as she motioned for him to continue out of the hall.

5

"I WOULD LIKE to finish this today if you please."

Aaron nodded and turned back to the wall, realizing he'd stayed with his head bowed much longer than was necessary. Princess Fen had gone from the hall, out somewhere with her gentleman suitor. He did his best to control his emotions, but it was hard. He was jealous of that man, jealous that he could walk with her, talk to her, would get the honor of knowing her in a way Aaron never could.

"I have all I need," Aaron said in distraction, not really paying attention to the short-tempered servant.

"But..." The servant looked at him and then the wall. "You didn't measure. You didn't write anything down. How can you say you have all you need? I will not be held responsible if you do not do your job."

Aaron wanted to tell the man to tie his mouth shut. A palace servant would hardly be held responsible for any mistake Aaron made. He'd been measuring tapestries for years. He knew what he was doing, and he hardly needed to use a measuring string for such an easy project.

"I said I've got all that I need," Aaron answered.

The servant huffed and led the way from the dining hall. Once outside, the man started to mumble. Aaron couldn't make out what he was saying but didn't really want to either.

As they walked out onto the pathways, he looked around for Fen. The day was warm and sweet, and the flowers bloomed in the brightness of the sun, but the winged *qizajian* were all gone. Feeling a pull, he turned off the path, quietly moving down a different route than the palace servant. He knew the man wouldn't look back to see if he followed.

Aaron slowed his step, moving lightly over the stones as he made his way toward the royal gardens. He wasn't sure how, but he knew she'd be there. All the servants spoke of how Princess Fen was to be married, how suitors had come to the palace for her hand. Was this noble her choice? And why did Aaron care?

Hearing feminine laughter, Aaron stepped off

the path and pressed close to the building where the emperor and empress slept. His hiding spot was shaded by the awning and hidden by a large leafy bush. Around the corner were the imperial gardens.

"You honor me with your compliments, Shing." The princess' voice drifted meekly on the breeze, stopping Aaron. His body stirred at the sound, arousing him with need. Her tone wasn't like that when she'd spoken to him. With him, there had been a light playfulness, if not subtle informality. He was a fool to let his body respond to her, but he could do little to stop it. He'd have a better chance in preventing his lungs from taking air.

"It is your beauty, Princess, that honors us all," her companion answered.

Aaron frowned, resisting the urge to roll his eyes heavenward. Such flowery words. Is that what she wanted? Is that who the princess was? Is that the type of man she wanted?

When Aaron fantasized about her, stroking his shaft to the image in his head, he wondered with a hint of fear what she would feel like compared to other women. Logically, he knew it'd be the same, but his mind imagined her sex so much softer, wetter, sweeter, tighter. Aaron suppressed a groan, shifting uncomfortably. His days at the palace were not the first time he'd thought of the princess in such a way but being so close to her made him feel almost criminal.

He kind of liked the sense of forbidden.

"You face is like the flower that draws the eye of mere mortals..." Shing continued, waxing poetic verse as he lavished compliment after compliment onto her. Fen giggled. Aaron crouched lower along the side of the building, his ears straining to hear every word.

The imperial gardens were a wondrous creation of what beauty had to offer. Large blue lookout trees grew in the corners, so strong, guards could step on their branches and follow the stair-step pattern carved around the trunk until they reached the top. From there, they could just see over the palace walls. The gardens were truly the most serene place in the palace, with open colonnades, flowering trees and shrubs, large boulders artfully placed and decorative red and gold fencing. There was even a small rock waterfall hidden in a corner. Aaron wouldn't have known it was there, except he stumbled upon it by accident during his morning exercise.

Fen and her suitor were partially hidden from view, but he found her instantly in the sea of garden colors. She was clad in the beautiful pink silk that he'd brought with him to the palace, and she looked as good in the pattern as he'd imagined she would when he had designed it for her. Sunlight shone over her head, outlining her slender form. Her hair gleamed just like finished silk and he bet it'd be just as soft to touch.

The noble next to her was every inch a gentleman in his dark blue silk tunic shirt and black pants. His hands threaded behind his rigid back. Ye Shing was a talker, as evident by the smooth richness of his words and the way he carried himself as if orating to a large hall. Aaron had dealt with his family before at Lady Hsin's, just as he'd dealt with many of the nobles who had sat at Fen's table—not that any of them seemed to remember him. It wasn't surprising. Nobles normally did not remember servants who were not their own.

"The blossoms fade with your nearness," Shing said.

Aaron looked down at his calloused hands. What did he know of speaking? Of pretty words? Unless it was to direct the factory workers at Lady Hsin's silk plantation, he hardly talked, and those words were hardly pretty.

"You speak very well." Fen smiled. She had such a sweet, pleasant smile. Aaron pulled back, hiding from view as Fen's words confirmed his suspicions about her. She'd like a man like Shing. "Your father tells me you are ready to take over his lands so that he may be at leisure."

Shing laughed. Aaron's frown deepened.

"My father says that, in hopes that you will be persuaded to think me too busy to be a husband and consider him instead, as he is titled, rich, and at leisure," Shing answered. "But if I were to marry, I would make time for a wife and she would not be expected to act like an old maid of four hundred."

"Hmm," Fen said, not answering him either way.

Aaron knew he should go before he was caught eavesdropping on the couple. Already he risked a great deal in just being where he was. A guard could be watching him from some hidden alcove. How would he explain spying on the princess?

Moving stealthily back to the path, he turned just in time to see Shing coming from the garden. His gut tightened, fearful that he'd been caught. He waited, his heart pounding, his whole-body stiff. The noble was alone and barely gave him a passing glance. Aaron relaxed and bowed in respect as Shing went by. The man didn't acknowledge him.

Fen would be alone in the garden. Aaron began walking toward her, pushing his shoulders back and lifting his jaw. He'd just walk and hope she noticed him. This wouldn't be the first time he'd tried such a technique. He'd put himself in her path often, hoping in vain that she would give him a look, a smile, a single word. So far, she hadn't seemed to notice, but that didn't stop him from trying.

"*Ni*, wait!"

Aaron stopped, turning to see Shing coming back down the path. He tensed. Had he done something to give himself away? Without speaking, he bowed his head in respect.

Shing came close, his tone low as he said, "The princess would like some *shui guo cha*. Would you please fetch it for her and bring it to the garden for us?"

The words were polite, but there was no doubt he was being ordered to do it. Aaron thought about telling the man he didn't work at the palace, but he doubted Shing would care. He'd only say that all men were subject to the wish of the princess, and he'd be right.

"*Xiexie ni*," Shing said, patting him on the arm as he hurried back toward the garden. "I appreciate it."

"No problem," Aaron mumbled as he headed back toward the dining hall to fetch the princess' tea.

6

FEN LOOKED at Zhang An as Shing walked away. "What are you doing, following us? I can't concentrate with you talking over him, let alone keep a straight face."

"Your eyes are the stars? Your lips are pink petals?" An snorted. "I've heard better prose from a *ch'ang shih*."

"Nice, Grandmother," Fen drawled sarcastically. "I'm sure Shing would appreciate you comparing him to a death-breathing corpse. Really, you should take it easier on the suitors. They're not that bad."

"What do you care if I tease Ye Shing? He's not for you," An assured her. "Not one of them is. They're unworthy to even consider marrying you."

"Ah, thanks Grandmother," Fen said, her tone

not lessening in the sarcasm. "How can you be so sure?" Fen asked, teasing. "Shing is very wealthy."

"You are wealthier," An said, floating idly above Fen. Her feet wiggled in the air for no apparent reason.

"And he is handsome." Fen moved to a bench and sat. She reached to cup two fingers around a flower, petting its silky white texture with her thumb. The blossom was pretty. She loved the gardens. They were so peaceful.

"Not so handsome as others." An's body fluttered as a breeze stirred. She glided to the bench and sat.

"Refined." Fen studied the flower, not really seeing it.

"Overrated," An whispered, the breeze caused by the word stirring the hair near her ear. Fen shivered.

"Charming." She let go and turned to the spirit. An's face was close, her nose almost touching Fen's.

"Practiced." An lifted her hand to Fen's cheek, moving gracefully to press her face to her grand-daughter's. Fen couldn't feel the touch, save for a faint coolness to her skin. "Learned."

Fen sighed. She was inclined to agree with her great-grandmother, but she wouldn't admit it and give the woman the satisfaction of hearing it.

An pulled back, her eyes almost sad. Fen knew

her grandmother missed the sensation of touch. She could feel but not as the living did—not unless she were to possess someone who was alive.

"There is something to be said for men who are not so noble." An wiggled her brows mischievously.

"*Hao.*" Fen laughed, tossing up her hands. "Okay, okay. I know you don't want me to marry anyone my mother picks out for me."

An grinned.

"Now, which ancestor did you say was watching us?"

"Ancestor?" An asked. "I didn't say an ancestor."

"*Shi,* you did." Fen nodded. "You said, 'He's watching you'."

"And he was." An waved her hand in circles, watching the trail of her ghostly gown.

"Who?" Fen grew mildly alarmed.

"The sexy man from the dining hall." An motioned to the side of the building. "The one who looks like he could show a woman a good—"

"Piers Aaron?" Fen's heart picked up a few beats.

"You know him?" An's transparent eyes glimmered with light for a moment.

"He saved my life," Fen said, breathless. "I mean, I believe he did." She quickly explained the fire to the woman, having intended to tell her anyway. After speaking with her brothers, she began to doubt it was anything more than a dream and hardly deemed it an urgent conversation. "Do you think he'll come over?"

An quirked a brow. "You're glowing."

Fen looked at her hands. "I'm...not."

"You are," An declared, pointing at her. "You're attracted to him. I was only teasing, but you *are* attracted to him. I can see why. He's—"

"I'm not," Fen continued to protest weakly. "How can I be? I'm drowning in suitors. I don't need any more."

"Swim to shore," An said wryly.

"Mother would not approve." As soon as she said it, Fen wished she could take the words back. An was the last person she wanted to say anything adverse to about her mother.

"*Wode tian*, what's he doing back?" An demanded.

Fen turned to see Shing.

"He didn't even bring your tea," An continued. Fen tried to ignore her as she forced a pleasant expression on her face. "Ask him to go back. Only this time, have him bring *po*—"

"I'm not drinking liquor this early in the day," Fen hissed out of the corner of her mouth.

"It's for me," An said. "If I have to listen to more

of his poetry, I'll need to be drunk."

Fen tilted her head to the side in question as she looked at Shing. "Were they out of tea?"

"A servant will bring it," Shing explained.

Pity, she thought, hoping he wouldn't recite another poem to her. Her smile widening, she said, "Perfect, *xiexie.* Thank you."

AARON CARRIED the tray before him, his stomach in knots at having to serve the princess in such a capacity. Of course, it was his luck that none of the servants was available to bring Princess Fen tea. They were still serving the royal table in the dining hall, so he was obliged to lend a hand. There was nothing wrong with laboring, he knew that, but still he was embarrassed. He didn't want her looking at him like a servant, even if that is all he could ever be to her.

Keeping his eyes on the tray, he watched to make sure he didn't drop the delicate teapot. Normally, he was agile, but nerves caused him to be less so.

Then he saw her standing in the garden, surrounded by pink, and he stopped thinking. He was drawn to her, his feet walking toward her with a mind of their own. Her eyes met his and he couldn't speak when his mouth opened.

"Piers Aaron," Princess Fen said, her pretty expression changing some when she saw him. She looked surprised. Shing turned around to look at him, a smile falling as his eyes hardened slightly. It was a subtle gesture, but one Aaron caught.

"Princess," Aaron was compelled to answer her, bowing over the tray.

"Ah, *xiexie ni*," Shing thanked him as he took the tray.

Aaron bowed his head and moved to take a step back so he could leave them.

"Wait," the princess said. Aaron stopped moving. This was the second time she'd commanded him in such a way. "When you're finished with the palace silks, I'd like to speak to you about an order. Please find me when it is convenient for you."

"Very good, Princess," Aaron said, taking a step back. He peeked up through his lashes to see her staring at him. His heart skipped a beat.

Shing stepped to the side, blocking her from view. Aaron stood, knowing that he'd been dismissed. He took a step back, watching the couple. Taking another, he backed away slowly, until he could no longer see them.

IT WAS evening before Aaron was able to pull away from his duties at the palace to meet Princess Fen. He thought about her all day, ever since he'd left the gardens. Though he went to work for her, it was still a reason to be in her presence and he gladly took it. His hands shook with the idea of taking her measurements. He never used the string measuring device, but with her he would—just to have reason to be near her. They did have her dress sizes on file, but it wouldn't hurt to be thorough.

The others that he'd brought with him from Lady Hsin's to help him work were busy sewing and designing for the empress. It was only reasonable that he went to Princess Fen alone, since they were occupied. It only took one of them to write down an order. Besides, he reasoned, Fen had asked for him to come. To send any other would be to disobey.

He hefted the book of silk samples under his arm, adjusting the great weight of it. Walking faster, his heart thumped a little harder than usual. So as not to embarrass himself, he'd also found pleasure at his own hand in the decontaminator unit in his guest room. Self-release was bittersweet in comparison to the real thing.

He neared her private quarters. Feeling very much like a thief sneaking into the treasure house, he glanced around. A guard looked at him from across the long path, taking him in curiously before turning away. Aaron did his best to appear nonchalant as he entered the building which would take him to Fen's private chamber.

A combination of anticipation, nervousness and excitement filled him. His hand shook as he lifted it before her door to knock. Hesitating, he took a deep breath, forcing all emotion from his face. Part of him screamed to turn back, that he'd insult her, embarrass himself, or worse, do something he'd regret. Even as he knew he should leave and send someone else in his stead, his hand fell forward against the door, hitting the wood softly.

"Enter," the princess' voice called from inside.

Aaron opened the door, licking his lips as he tried to force his gaze down to the floor. It was hard not to peek at her when in her presence. He entered her bedchamber from the hall. The guest rooms were set up the same way—bedrooms by the door, with adjoining chambers for leisure and bathing. Though, the guest rooms were much smaller than those of the royal family.

He finally allowed himself to look up. Instantly, his eyes were drawn to the bed. It was empty, but the soft silk of the coverlet looked crumpled, as if she'd recently lain upon it. How he wished he could've been with her, her soft body surrounded by silk. Swallowing, he tried to force such things from his mind. But how could he help it? Fen was exquisite.

"I'm in here," Fen called, stopping him from thinking anything further.

Aaron walked to her living chamber, stepping through the thin open door. His hand tightened on his sample book, his fingers working against the thick binding. Inside were different silk color swatches and gown patterns. It was his personal book, a collection he'd put together over the years of his best designs—both in gowns and silk embroidery. Being at Lady Hsin's, he made it a point to learn all aspects of the silk business. Designs were just one of his more favorite areas of work.

"I was beginning to think you had forgotten me," Fen said. "Either that, or my mother is keeping you extra busy."

He found her lounging on a low couch. Her feet were on the floor, but her body rested to the side. A fire glowed in a small firepot, outlining her body with a soft orange. His desires stirred.

So much for self-release.

"Princess, please forgive my tardiness," he said, automatically.

"There is nothing to forgive," she answered easily, her voice like music. "I'm just grateful that you could manage to fit me in at all. I know how much the empress' order must be filling your days with work. But just knowing that Lady Hsin's beautiful silks are so close, I couldn't resist ordering some for myself. She designs the most wonderful patterns."

Aaron suppressed a frown at that. Lady Hsin didn't design so much as a curve on a flower. She didn't even come to the production house, or the plant, or the fields. He did all that for her. The only time the workers saw her was when she had guests.

Aaron wisely didn't correct the princess' assumption. If he did, and word got back to Hsin, he'd be reprimanded and would most likely lose his job.

"It is an honor to work for her," Aaron agreed.

"How shall we start?" Fen asked, standing. "Is here all right?"

Aaron gulped and nodded. The princess was scantily clad. The dark blue silk robe was long, but the thin material clung to her perfect body until even the subtle press of her nipples showed in glorious outline. There was no design to the plain material, but the fact only added to the seductiveness of the outfit, as there were no distracting patterns to hide her shape.

Silk...delicate...flower...lips like petals...

He tried to think of the poetry to describe her as Shing had in the garden, only to be at a loss. Mere words did not do her justice.

Her shiny hair was down around her shoulders, framing her perfect face. He looked at her mouth, full lips that could make any man ache. His hand trembled on the book and he knew he needed to set it down before he dropped it on the floor.

"May I?" he asked, motioning to a low table.

Fen gestured toward it. "Please."

To reach the table, he had to go near her. He did, slowly moving under the duress of his aroused body.

Kneeling, he set the book down. Her legs were close and he glanced over, seeing the outline of a thigh.

Tianna, to touch that thigh.

Slowly, she knelt beside him. Aaron opened the book, asking, "Did the princess have anything particular in mind?"

"Gowns, robes, sashes," she answered, her voice so soft he imagined it to be breathless, "intimates."

Aaron's cock twitched to attention. He really should have sent another in his stead.

"Too much?" she asked. "I can order less if you don't have time."

"No. It is fine." What else could he say? It wasn't wise to refuse a member of the royal family.

"Good. I'm glad you can indulge me. Clothes are my weakness, and this silk," she paused, reaching to touch a patch of dark green with the head of a phoenix on it, "is just too tempting. Take care how much you show me, or I might just order it all."

Aaron reached for his belt and pulled out a small electronic clipboard for notes. Making a notation that the order was for Princess Fen, he set down the writing wand and turned expectantly to the book. "Should we start with gowns?"

"Please," said Fen.

"Is there a special occasion...?" He couldn't finish, not wanting to hear of a wedding.

"No, no occasion," she said. "Just your everyday ceremonies."

"But, the empress mentioned..." Again, he couldn't say the words.

Fen laughed. "I assure you. What the empress says and what I say are two different things. There are no occasions in which I should think on."

Aaron felt relieved. She hadn't chosen a husband. Though, why should he care either way?

"Oh, I like this," Fen said, touching a piece of dark red. She unclipped it from the book and held it to her cheek. "What do you think? Does the color suit me?"

At her invitation to look, Aaron turned his eyes to her. He looked at where she held it to her cheek and weakly nodded that it did.

"Perfect, I'll take it in..." She pulled a bulk of the pages forward to where design plates were normally placed in the back of the book. Pointing to a dress with long, draping sleeves and a high collar, she finished, "This."

Aaron wrote down the request.

The princess turned back to the front of the book, put the silk sample back and continued to browse. Pointing at three swatches in turn, she said, "Robe, robe, sash for a gown. You pick the final designs. I'm sure you know more about this than I do. Just make something suitable. I love surprises."

Aaron wrote those orders down as well.

"Oooh, I like this." She took off a piece of dark blue embroidered with tiny gold swirls. It was a more masculine design, but anything would look good on the princess. "What do you think of this on me?"

Aaron again glanced over, thinking to see it by her cheek. Instead, she held it to her neck, close to the V in her robe. His mouth went dry as he looked at her slender throat. The material blended with the color she was wearing, and he pretended to study it against her when really he was doing his best not to look at her breasts.

"The gold too much?" she asked softly. *Wode tian,* but her voice drove him to distraction. He was about to answer, when she drew the silk to his cheek. "Hmm, it would look better on you. It matches your eyes."

Aaron drew his gaze down. His body hummed. The silk was still warm from her flesh and it was as if she touched him. Reaching for the book, he took off a sample of lighter blue. "Perhaps this?"

Fen pushed her cheek out in offering, blinking prettily. "How does it look?"

Aaron lifted the piece with a sense of the surreal. The princess was so close he could detect her light perfume. She smelled like the garden wind—fresh and sweet with the hint of flowers. He touched it to her cheek, well aware of how alone they were. Was the princess telling him something by her actions? Or was his hopeful mind grasping at what wasn't there?

"Beautiful," he said, before he could stop the word.

Fen smiled, and he pulled the silk back. "I'll take it. You have good taste, Aaron. Why don't you pick the gown for it? I trust your judgment."

Aaron nodded, trying to focus on his work. They went through several more patterns and samples until Fen felt she'd ordered enough gowns and robes to satisfy her. Once, while flipping through the book, her hand brushed close to his. It was a light touch, but one he knew would haunt him when he left. As he pretended to study the swatches, he got glimpses of her body—the sweet curve of her chest with nipples pressed against the silk, the long length of her graceful arm. He watched her small hands on the book, caressing the silk as she followed patterns with her delicate fingertips.

Aaron turned the page, getting to the lighter, thinner swatches for nightclothes. Fen hummed softly to see them, reaching to caress them as she had the others. The patterns were simpler than the gowns had been, but she still fingered each of them.

"You have shown yourself a great judge of women's fashion," Fen said. "I'm inclined to bow to your opinion in this matter as well."

Aaron swallowed, tortured by the odd sense of foreplay he felt was happening, yet knew could not be. Maybe he read too much into her actions. And yet her smiles were such that if they'd been on anyone else, he'd have taken the lead in the game of seduction. But Fen was a princess, and he couldn't, *shouldn't*, think such wickedly erotic thoughts about her. To think of her wrapped in the thin fabrics before them, to see her in the thin gown she now wore, was agony.

He reached for a pink swatch. "I think this one."

"I like that one," she said.

"And, this." He touched a green.

"Mmm, *ke ai*," she agreed. "An excellent choice."

"This one." He pointed to a dark red.

"*Hao.*"

"A dark blue with red flowers." The silk wasn't in the book, but it was in his head.

"I don't see that one?" She reached to flip the page.

"Green butterflies on dark blue," he continued. "I will have it drawn especially for you."

She didn't answer.

"How many do you desire?" he asked, hearing the huskiness to his own tone.

"One more," she whispered.

"Soft pink, with a darker pink shade of lotus flowers." How great she would look in it. He could see it now, her body on the bed, the pink silk pushed up around her thighs, barely guarding her sex from view. "They will take some time to finish, but I could have them to you in a few months after leaving the palace."

"Divine," she answered. "I should love that."

Each time he forced himself to look, it was harder. He needed to get out of there before he did something stupid.

Reaching for the book, he slammed it shut a little too abruptly and reached for his clipboard, making the necessary notes before setting it on the sample book.

"If that will be all," he said, trying to force his legs to stand. They wobbled beneath him, his knees weak.

"No, actually, there is one more thing." Fen slowly stood next to him. "The gown I had on earlier today. It was beautiful, and I have no complaints about the workmanship, but I am afraid it was too tight."

Aaron couldn't resist, he looked up at her. She ran her hands over her waist.

"It hurt to breathe," she explained, "and left marks upon my flesh, here." She skimmed her ribs near her breasts. "And here." She ran her hands down to her hips, tapping the front of her pelvic bone. "I think it would be best to have myself re-measured."

The empress had ordered the gown made a half-size smaller than Fen's measurements. He knew he should say something, but he couldn't. He reached for his waist, pulling out the measuring string. Fen straightened her back and dropped her hands to her sides.

He turned toward her, walking on his knees as he stayed kneeling at her feet. Aaron reached to measure her hip to the floor. This is what he'd wanted, the excuse to touch her, but the pain of denial was strong. His head was clouded, and it took all his willpower to remain calm. He pressed his fingers to her warm hip, feeling it intimately beneath the thin silk. He had to look three times before he comprehended the measurement. Turning, he wrote it down, only to move back to find she'd adjusted her weight. Her thighs were parted slightly and closer to him than before. He took a long, deep breath, getting an intimate hint of her body's secret fragrance.

Was this really happening? Was Fen really inviting his touch? Or was she teasing him with his own desires? Bored noblewomen had teased him in such a way before, testing him, trying to see if he would break. To them it was a game, one they never thought to finish. Then again, there were those bored women who did wish to continue, whose fathers kept them locked tight in their homes away from common men. Which was Fen? Was she playing the game or was she inviting him to be her lover?

"You hesitate," she said.

Aaron reached forward, trying to rush. He stood and took a few more measurements, mindlessly writing them down—the width of her waist and neck, the length of her arms. When moving to reach around her back to measure her chest, he felt her lean forward. She sighed, the warm breath a small caress against his neck and ear.

Bumps sprouted over his flesh, causing him to

shiver. His cock was hard, strained from the endless time in her company.

He pulled the string, moving it so it lay across her chest. Her nipples were hard peaks beneath the silk and he couldn't resist letting the string rub across them as he adjusted to measure.

She gasped, wiggling just a little.

"Perhaps," she said, reaching for her waist, "this will make your task easier."

Aaron felt his entire world spin out of control as she said the words *make your task easier.* There was a hidden meaning buried inside her sultry tone.

Fen pulled the belt at her waist. He dropped the string so it fell from around her. She wiggled her shoulders, forcing the thin robe to slither off her body.

Aaron had never wanted to sink his cock into a woman so badly in his life. Pert, round breasts drew his eyes, leading him down the flat plains of her stomach to the small thatch of hair between her perfect thighs. His breathing deepened as he detected the smallest glistening near the curls of her nether region.

"I want the measurements to be right," she told him. Her lips parted. "I would have my gowns fit."

Taking her cue, he reached around her again. He

turned his face toward her, gauging her reaction as he let his fingers purposefully touch her naked arm. She closed her eyes, breathing intensely. Aaron brought the string around her upper body, beneath her raised arms to her breasts. The backs of his hands touched the mounds, and she gasped, arching slightly.

Not reading the string, he said, "I've got what I need for the gowns."

Fen took the string from him and eyed him carefully. "My turn. It is my wish that you make yourself a tunic out of the blue and gold. The one that matches your eyes. Absorb the cost into my bill."

Aaron would never do such a thing but kept quiet. The princess reached for him and he stiffened. She boldly touched his chest, running her hands over the plain brown tunic he wore.

"Brown does not suit you," she said. "It's too plain a color."

"It suits a worker," he corrected.

"But not you." She pursed her lips, giving a cute little pout. "Take it off."

Aaron hesitated, but when she arched a brow, he obeyed, opening the front and slipping it off his shoulders.

"Mmm," she moaned. It was a small, sexy noise in the back of her throat. "This is much better."

Her eyes turned down and she gasped lightly to see his erection straining against his pants. Aaron knew he had no reason for shyness when it came to that part of his nature, and it was in fact one of the reasons he had the lovers he did in the past. A small twinge echoed over his heart to think that Fen might use him as the others had—not that he hadn't found his fair amount of pleasure in the past. But the desires of the flesh were a sad comparison to the joys of the heart.

To his surprise and carnal delight, she took the string to his pants. The back of her hand bumped against his balls as she held one end of the measuring string near the root of his shaft. The material of his pants still separated their skin, but that didn't stop her exploration. Drawing the string upward, she stopped near the tip.

The surreal fact that a naked princess was measuring his cock shook him to the core. Material separated their flesh, but it was enough of a caress to cause his hips to jerk.

"*Tianna,*" she said in awe. A base masculine pride welled inside him at her exclamation. She licked her lips as the string fell to the floor. "You're so big and strong." Fen touched his chest, rubbing it. His small nipples hardened as she stroked over them, exploring each curve of his upper body. "All these huge muscles." She drew her hand slowly down to his waistband. "And this muscle, just as big and strong. Is it as used to working hard? Or do you neglect its exercise."

He couldn't help the small grin that crossed his lips, even as he was shocked. There was nothing flowery or poetic about her words, and yet he found them much more erotic than a thousand sonnets. He wouldn't have guessed the Zhang princess capable of such mild vulgarities. He rather enjoyed them.

Her hand slipped beneath the material of his breeches, moving to wrap around his erection. "Mmm, you must exercise it, for it is so very hard and thick. Do you have a lover?"

He shook his head in denial. It was the truth. He hadn't had a lover for some time.

"A woman waiting for you?"

Again, he shook his head.

"Ah, then you must work out alone." A pretend look of sorrow crossed her face and she pouted her lower lip.

Aaron groaned, still not moving to touch her. He wanted to. *Tian xiao de*, how he wanted to. But he held back, part of him still restrained by the fact that she was a princess and had not given him express permission to react.

She jerked his pants off his hips and pushed them down. They fell to the floor, pooling at his feet until he was as naked as she. Biting her lip, she looked down at the weapon she held in her hand.

"Mmm, hard, yet smooth like silk," she purred. Her hips wiggled back and forth ever so slightly. "You forgot one measurement, Piers Aaron. Surely you don't wish to slack in your duties."

Princess Fen leaned forward, lightly brushing her mouth against his.

This was like a dream. Surely, he couldn't be awake.

Her lips parted as she leaned into him. Aaron slowly reached for her, letting his hands feel the soft skin of her sides.

How? Why? Surely he'd done nothing to deserve such heavenly delights.

So many questions filtered through his brain, but he couldn't stop to ask them. Her tongue pushed boldly forward between his lips, licking the seam until he opened his mouth to allow her access. Uncertain, he began to move against her, every ounce of reason dying in the arms of pleasure.

Her kiss became more insistent as she touched

the sides of his face, pulling him against her. She was like holding a bolt of warm silk against his body. He adjusted his hips, pressing his erection into her stomach. Hard nipples grazed his chest as she wiggled against him.

This can't be happening. Wode tian, this can't be happening.

The dam of self-control within him broke. Fierce with passion, he grabbed her to his chest, crushing her against him. His hands roamed over her back, tangling in her hair as he reveled in the fruits of her seduction.

8

Fen tried to gasp as Aaron's passion turned from accepting to commanding, but the press of his lips, sawing suddenly against hers, stopped any sound from escaping. She became lightheaded, her lungs burning for air.

When he first came to her room, distant and aloof, she wasn't sure she could go through with her plan to get him into bed. But she'd wanted him and intended to have him. When she saw him earlier in the gardens, holding the tray, she'd liked it. In a perverse way, she enjoyed the idea of him serving her —in all ways.

Seducing him gave her a thrill, especially since she didn't know if he wanted her. No man had ever been so hard to read, especially when she gave all the signs. But then, she'd never seduced a commoner before. She had hoped he was into her, but until she was sure, she took it slow—sitting close to him, wearing the slinky robe, holding the swatches against her skin to draw his eyes where she wished them to go.

With each passing attempt, she saw his eyes straying a few seconds longer to her breasts, sensed that he was aroused by the invisible, electrifying pull between them, but still he hadn't made a single move to touch her.

With the men she'd known in the past, at least from what she could remember, after she dropped a few hints, they took the lead and made the first official move. When Aaron had touched her to take her measurements, she'd been sure he'd grow bolder. Her skin had lit on fire and her thighs had been so tight with need. As he knelt, she imagined grabbing his head and smothering his face against her sex, demanding his thick, calloused fingers ram up into her so she could find her release. His nearness is what caused such stinging sexual discomfort. It was only right that he be the one to relieve her of it. But he kept working, despite her obvious hints.

In the end, she couldn't stop what happened. She was going to have him. She *had* to have him.

Now, as he finally took over, his rough hands seeming to touch everywhere at once, she trembled with relief and a sense of fear in the unknown. He wasn't refined like a gentleman, nor was he overly tender when he ground his stiff cock into her. Hard muscles strained under her hands as he reached to lift her up by the hips. She held onto his shoulders. His mouth left hers, moving to capture a breast between his aggressive teeth. Her legs automatically wrapped around his waist for balance.

Hot, blinding pleasure exploded over her chest from where he sucked against her, shooting like laser beams throughout her body, centering in the nerve-endings in her sex. She ached to be filled, wanting to feel his thick, long inches inside her.

The liquid heat of his mouth only continued, moving to the other breast. He bit her nipple, sending a hard jolt through her stomach. It had been so long since she'd felt pleasure and never had it been so intense. Her heart pounded heavily, echoing with the low sound of his moans within her ears.

Aaron set her down on the floor once more. His dark blue eyes burned with passion as he looked directly at her. Fen took a step back, feeling very small under his intent gaze. His hands followed her, keeping hold of her hips so she couldn't get away.

The length of his arousal stood between them like a sword.

His voice hoarse, he said, "Don't stop."

Suddenly, she didn't feel like a princess. She felt like how normal women must feel. It was a freeing sensation.

"Take me as you would one of your women," she said. "I want to know what it is like."

His eyes clouded briefly at that but were soon blazing once more. Before she could comprehend the expression, he took her arm and spun her around. Fen gasped. His hard erection pressed along the cheeks of her ass. The table was in front of her and he stepped forward, forcing her toward it. When they reached it, he pushed on her back, bending her forward so that her palms were down flat. Her head angled toward the floor and her butt was in the air.

He bumped her ass with his hips, urging her forward still. She climbed onto the table on her hands and knees. A thick thigh nudged her legs open from behind and a hand moved to guide the tip of his shaft to her opened sex. The first intimate brush along her folds made her stomach clench. And then he pushed, firm and sure, as he pried her body open to him.

There was no gentle probing, no easy foreplay to

make sure she was stretched and ready. It didn't matter. The pressure of him inside her, gliding forward in her cream, was pure heaven.

Fen's fingers curled around the edge of the table. The hard plank of wood stung her knees. Aaron held her hips, pulling her back, controlling her, moving her as he pushed himself deeper still.

So long it had been since she'd had sex, and the potency of those celibate years now gathered in her awakened body. With a jerk, he brought himself to the hilt. Fen moaned, clutching the table, and he pushed her forward only to yank her roughly back. His body hit deep inside hers. Fen loved the sheer naughtiness of their position. Never had a man taken her like this, so hard and wild, and she couldn't help thinking that commoners definitely made better lovers. The rough pull of his hands, the strong look of his work-hewn body, the gruff sound of his breaths as he moved in and out, in and out, harder, faster, they all turned her on more.

Pressure built, the ache of oncoming pleasure centering where he touched. Aaron slipped a hand down over her stomach, moving to probe her clit with his finger. She jerked in response and he pumped faster.

"*Shi, shi,*" she cried, "yes, yes!"

It was close, so close, the final release.

"Ah," she gasped, her whole body tensing as the waves of climax took over. Aaron moved a few more times, before he too grunted the height of his pleasure.

Moments later, he withdrew and supported her arm as she crawled off the table.

Now that she'd achieved her goal, much to the gratification of her body, she wasn't sure how to act. Some of her confidence faded. When she turned, Aaron was getting dressed, pulling his breeches up from the floor.

Prompted by his actions, she quickly slipped into her robe. Sex had been pleasurable but not intimate. How could it be when she hadn't looked deep into his eyes, felt the full length of his body to hers? Once dressed, she turned to face him, smiling softly.

"If you require nothing else..." His voice tapered off. Aaron reached for the sample book and his electronic clipboard full of notations.

"This wasn't required," Fen said, not sure whether to be hurt by the assumption. He acted as if she often commanded servants to pleasure her. "I didn't mean for you to think you had to... That I was ordering you to..."

His dark eyes met hers, and she felt as if she

couldn't breathe. He seemed to have that effect on her.

"I wanted this," she said. "I hope you wanted it to."

Slowly, as if debating the intelligence of his answer, he nodded.

"When you came, before," she motioned to her room, remembering how he came in on her. "Thank you."

"I did nothing."

"You came to my rescue," she said lightly, stepping a little closer before stopping. "*Xiexie*. Thank you."

He nodded once. "I think it might be best if I go. The others will wonder why I took so long, and you..." He closed his eyes and took a deep breath. "You have suitors here for your hand. It wouldn't do if they were to suspect that we..."

She nodded, understanding what he was saying. Finishing for him, she whispered, "If we were involved."

"You have a reputation. You are a princess. I'm a—"

Fen cut him off by placing her hand to his warm mouth. "I would like to see you again."

He didn't give her the rush of agreement she

hoped for. Instead, he seemed ready to deny the request.

"It's not an order," she clarified. "I don't want you to feel as if you are forced to be in my company."

"Your company is hardly unpleasant, Princess," he assured her. "I, too, would like to see you."

Fen smiled, never realizing that her stomach had been so knotted as she waited for the barest hint that he wanted her. "I have a full day tomorrow with the..." She couldn't say the word. "I have a full day."

He nodded, and she got the impression he didn't want to hear her talk of the other men either, just as she didn't want to say the words.

"But I'll find a way to sneak off. I'll find you," she assured him.

Leaning forward, he pressed a hard kiss to her lips before moving toward the door.

Fen watched him leave, wanting to beg him to stay. But he was right. It wouldn't be fitting for her to take a lover when men were here vying for her attentions—especially when those men were nobles and her lover was far from it. The scandal would mortify her family and damage her reputation. She would have to be careful. The idea that they tried so hard to pretend like they were equals on this planet, only to care about such things as social class when it came to marriage, wasn't lost on her. It wasn't fair, but it was what it was.

Fen smiled, feeling as if she played a game whose prize was pleasure like she'd never known. There was a sense of danger in the forbidden act of what she'd done, what she was doing.

Smiling, feeling more alive than any other time in her life, she walked to the bed. An ache filled her, a longing to know more of Aaron, a longing to have him hold her close throughout the night. The unrealized desire would only make the next time they came together all the sweeter. Anticipation was a powerful aphrodisiac.

Still smiling, she closed her eyes.

"Lights off." Her room darkened at the voice command and with the liquid numbness of aftermath still in her limbs, she fell into a deep, untroubled sleep.

Aн! The pain was too much. She had looked at him, spoken to him, but she didn't see him. Her eyes didn't burn, not like his heart did.

The man rocked faster, twitching with irritation and impatience. He'd looked at her, seen her, but she didn't see him, not really.

Why had his ancestors forsaken him? He left them offerings, left the gifts, left his blood. Why? Why?

He was so sure when invitations to the palace to court the princess were sent out that it was time for Princess Fen to be his wife. But she didn't respond to him, at least nothing beyond politeness. She gave as much to all the others at her table. How could she see him, and only him, when she had to look around the heads of so many?

Shi, it wasn't her fault she couldn't see him. There were too many distractions at the emperor's palace, too many men vying for her attention.

He must get rid of them—somehow. Murder was too foul, too crass for a man like him. However, there was art in deceit, in manipulation. He could make them want to leave, manipulate the situation until they fled the palace and only he and his love were left.

His heart was flooded with passion, so full it was near bursting like a dam against a swollen river. Rocking back and forth, he closed his eyes. His arms wrapped around his knees, holding tight.

"If she will not burn, make her drown—drown in her passions for me. I beg of you, blessed ancestors, make her drown in her passion for me until she can feel nothing else."

He rocked faster, meditating on his desires as his cock hardened. He yearned that his wishes would finally come true. No man had ever suffered as he now suffered. It was unbearable, the love he felt, the heavy lust pushing from his hips. Too long he'd seen her, watched her, wanted her, only to be denied his chances to win her. No longer would he be in the shadows. No longer would he be denied what he wanted. Princess Fen would be his.

"Flood her body. Make her feel the suffocation. Let her not breathe until I breathe. Drown her for me, blessed ancestors, make her drown."

"Аннн!"

Fen's arms and legs flailed in the air as she plummeted off the small bridge. It arched over the Enchanted River, a small stream that flowed within the palace walls. With a splash that stung her back, she hit the water, dipping beneath the surface into the icy depths.

For a stunned moment, she couldn't believe that the old bridge had given out. The rail had seemed so sturdy. How could such a thing crack?

Pumping her arms, she pulled her body toward the surface. Above her, she heard a shout. Lord He, the elderly Singhai nobleman, looked down at her from the edge. Around her, trees lined both sides of the stream. This area of the palace looked more like wilderness.

"*Ni mei shi ba?*" he asked, his tone hard.

Fen frowned, even as she sputtered to get the

water out of her mouth. Was she all right? Did she look like she was all right? She pumped her arms, at first severely annoyed at the Singhai nobleman for merely standing there staring at her, until she realized she had greater concerns than just being wet and cold. The weight of the thick embroidered gown started to pull her down again. She worked her arms harder and faster. The dress shouldn't have been that heavy when wet.

"*Qing bang-zhu wo,*" Fen yelled. "Help me."

Lord He leaned over the side, waving his hand. "Swim to the shore."

Fen tried, but she couldn't. The man above her didn't move as he continued to watch.

"Swim," he ordered, as if she were a soldier. "Move your arms. Swim to shore."

Fen tried to answer that she couldn't—when what felt like a hand gripped her ankle and jerked her down. She sank, pulled lower into the river. Of all the years they'd floated above the gentle waves, she never imagined any part of it being so deep as to drag her down with the current. Her ground shoe slipped off as she kicked, and she finally was able to pull her body up. Gasping, she took a lungful of air, enough to croak, "Lord He, help me, please!"

Another sweeping current grabbed her, and she

was pulled down once more. The cold water invaded every pore, making her limbs numb and her head light.

As she fought to survive, all she could think was how she cursed her mother for making her walk with Lord He in the first place.

10

TO THE WATER...

Aaron dropped the bolt of silk he was carrying, as the urge to run toward the Enchanted River overtook him. He wasn't sure what made the thought pop into his head, but somehow he knew Fen would be there, and that she needed him.

Run faster. She needs you.

Obeying the inner voice, he took off into a sprint, leaving the material where it lay on the dirty ground. The paths along the river's edge were long and he wasn't sure how he knew which way to turn.

Left, the voice in his head commanded. *Faster.*

Aaron ran harder, sprinting as he heard a man shout, "Swim to shore. Use your arms."

The pathway forked in two directions. One way

led to the pompous old Lord He. The nobleman stood up on the old bridge, not moving as he leaned against the rail and looked toward the water. Aaron's gaze followed where the nobleman was looking. Rings traveled over the rippling surface of the river.

Suddenly, a hand came from the depths, reaching for the sky. Fen's head soon followed as she gasped, "Lord He, help me!"

The Singhai nobleman didn't move to go to the princess' aid. Lord He might have been old, but he wasn't too old to swim to the woman's rescue. Any true man would at least try or drown with her. Disgust curled in Aaron's stomach. Lord He might have money and power, but he was no gentleman. No man could stand by, screaming commands, while a woman died before him.

Taking only a second to assess the situation, Aaron grabbed his shirt and threw it over his head as he ran for the water, taking the path that led away from Lord He.

Years of playing in the creek near his village had made him a strong swimmer. Diving into the warm water, he stroked his arms, gliding easily to Princess Fen. He came up for air. Beneath him, the water was still and easy to maneuver. Aaron dove once more, seeing the shadows of Fen's movements. He grabbed her wrist and pulled. Her flesh was like ice beneath his fingers, a strange contrast to the warm river. It took a couple jerks, but he managed to free her from whatever trapped her. Hooking Fen beneath her arms, he swam with all his might toward shore.

There was no time for fear as he saved her. Aaron merely did what he had to do. But, as he pulled her to the safety of shore, laid her on the path and watched her choke in a quivering breath, his stomach knotted, and he suddenly felt sick with the idea of what could have been. He glanced up to see Lord He coming for them at a clipped pace. Aaron wanted to hit the man for just passively watching as the princess drowned. He held back, the last thoughts of self-preservation keeping him from insulting a noble.

Fen's face was wet and pale and her skin was only just starting to warm. Even now, he felt unworthy of touching her. The night before had been magic, more than he'd ever dreamt possible. Princess Fen, for whatever reason, had chosen to be with him and had asked him to come back. It was clear she wanted to take him as a lover, for however long he was at the palace. Who was he to say no to such a plan?

If he tried, he knew he could discover her

motives. He was a commoner. She wanted to see what it would be like to have sex with a common man. He was a servant in her home. She had the power to command him to silence. He was lower than she in class, and if he was to speak of what happened, none would believe him, and those who pretended to listen would only do so out of the desire to spread nasty rumors about Fen and her family.

Aaron blocked all these truths from his mind, for what other reason could Princess Fen have chosen him? Heaven knew, a very big part of him didn't care what her reasons were. He wanted her. He'd held out for as long as he could during her seduction, but in the end, he couldn't stop from touching her any more than he could control the circumstance of his birth. All day he'd thought of her, torn with the knowledge that she was being courted by other men and elated by the promise of meeting her later. He took a small amount of satisfaction in knowing that while they courted her, *he* would be fucking her.

Looking up at Lord He, it took all his strength to keep his mouth shut. The man wasn't worthy to court her. His only qualification was that of his birth.

Fen coughed. Lord He frowned severely at him. Aaron realized his hands were on her shoulders and he quickly drew them away. Her face was so pale and he didn't want to leave her, but he had to. Breathing hard, more from the fear inside him than the exertion of swimming, he stood, leaning over to grab his shirt from the ground. Wet hair clung to his skin as he slipped the dry shirt over his head.

Lord He folded his hand in front of his stout body, not moving to help the princess up.

"Aaron?" Fen mumbled weakly. She held out her hand toward him.

"Princess," Lord He said. "Are you injured?"

Fen blinked, dropping her hand as she looked over to Lord He. She coughed again. Her eyes narrowed. "Aaron, please help me to my chambers. I don't feel like I can walk on my own."

"I will escort you as well," Lord He said, as if gracing Fen with his presence. Then nodding at Aaron, he ordered, "Boy, help her up."

Aaron's gut tightened at the command, but what could he say? He leaned over, gently pulling Fen to her feet. Her knees buckled and he instantly caught her, automatically swinging her into his arms. Lord He watched his every move and Aaron tried to act indifferent. With a nod, the nobleman ordered him to walk. Fen sighed, leaning her head to his shoulder. Her light weight and thin, cold body were hardly a burden as he climbed the slight incline up toward the main pathways, away from the secluded area of water. They walked in relative silence. Aaron wanted to ask her what happened but held back.

"*Xiexie ni,*" Fen whispered a few times, keeping her eyes closed. "Thank you."

When they passed another servant, Lord He told the man, "Fetch the palace physician. The princess fell into the river."

The servant obeyed.

"Put her here," Lord He ordered when they reached the royal sleeping chambers. He pointed right outside the front door. "I will escort her inside."

"I don't think she should walk," Aaron said, before he could stop himself.

"We do not require your opinion, boy," Lord He said sternly. "You may go. I said I would help her."

Aaron held her tighter. "And the princess doesn't require a heartless, pompous ass like you."

Lord He and Fen both gasped at the affront. Fen leaned away from his chest, staring at him.

"I will have you whipped for that, boy," Lord He promised. "You have no right to speak thus to me."

Aaron instantly knew his mistake. Lord He wasn't only a noble, he was a foreign noble, and one invited by the emperor to their territory.

When Fen didn't speak, he set her legs down, prepared to leave.

"Aaron saved my life, Lord He," Fen said softly, not meeting the nobleman's eyes. She swayed lightly on her feet but still proudly held her head up. "He will not be whipped."

"I demand—" Lord He began.

"You have no right to demand," Fen cut him off sharply, looking up to give the noble a hard stare. "Aaron, please, help me inside."

Lord He lifted his chin, refusing to bow as he stormed off. Fen swayed on her feet and Aaron instantly grabbed her elbow.

"You should not have defended me," Aaron said.

"Nonsense," Fen argued, walking inside with his help. "You defended *me*. Lord He *is* a pompous ass and I'll be glad to be rid of him."

Aaron smiled, holding the door for her. "But he is a guest of your father."

Fen returned his look with a shy smile of her own. "I like when you speak to me. Had I known merely falling into the river would have brought you to my side, I would've jumped in this morning. I missed you today. I looked for you."

"I've been busy overseeing the sewing of the tapestries for the dining hall." Aaron held open the door to her sleeping chambers, hesitating before going inside.

"You've brought me this far…" she said, letting her words taper off.

He led her inside, helping her to the bed. As she braced herself against the mattress, not crawling on top, he said, "You should get out of those wet clothes."

"I would much rather you got me out of them." She smiled, but the look was ruined when she started coughing.

"You're in no condition for such things," he scolded.

"I'll be fine after the medic comes," she assured him. "Promise me you'll come here later. Tonight. I want to be with you again."

"No, not here," he said. "I won't risk your reputation, and no one takes two nights to order gowns."

"The imperial gardens?" she asked, visibly shivering.

He frowned, trying to figure out where her clothes were kept. "No, your parents sleep near there. I don't think it would be safe."

"Where then?" she asked.

"You really need to get into bed. You're freezing cold." He went to her, trying to get her to lie down.

Her trembling hands touched his face. "Tell me where first."

"The, ah, weapons building," he said. "It should be empty. Now, lie down."

"I'll be there," she swore.

He made a move to answer, but the door to her chambers opened and the empress rushed inside, followed by several servants and the physician. Instantly, Aaron stepped back from Fen, bowing low, "It was my honor to be of service, Princess."

Fen nodded but didn't speak. The empress moved past him and the others crowded him until he was forced to leave. Going to Péng You Hall to dry off, he stopped only to tell one of the workers where to find the bolt of material he'd dropped on the ground.

Once alone, he smiled, elated that the princess wanted him as much as he wanted her.

11

FEN LOOKED up from the bed. Her wet clothes were gone and she was warming up under a tall stack of blankets her mother insisted on piling over her. The physician claimed the cold was from shock, even though Fen wasn't as convinced by it as he was. He checked her with his medical handheld and declared she would recover with some rest. When the young doctor left, her mother shooed the servants out of Fen's chambers.

Sitting on her bed, the empress touched her face. "You were very lucky Lord He was there to save you."

"What?" Fen tried to sit up.

The empress pushed her down, frowning at the attempt. "He told us everything that happened."

"That's not..." Fen shook her head. "He—"

"He also told us of Lady Hsin's worker's behavior. Don't worry, we will ensure the insolent man is thrown from the palace and Lady Hsin will be told of his poor manners."

"No, wait," Fen broke in. "*Aaron* saved me. Lord He just stood there watching me drown. Aaron dove in after me, pulled me out, and even carried me from the Enchanted River to here."

The Empress looked as if she didn't believe her daughter, or in the very least that Fen didn't know what she was talking about.

"Aaron *did* save me," Fen insisted.

Slowly, her mother nodded. "Lord He did not see it that way."

"He wouldn't." She quickly told her mother everything that had happened. Well, everything but their plans to meet later.

Her mother patted her cheek briefly. "Then it is well that you have other suitors to choose from. The emperor will see to it that Lord He leaves at once. It will cause problems with trade relations, but I will not have a man here who does not lift a finger to save my daughter. And to think, he lied to me about Aaron being contrary with him."

Fen swallowed. As much as she hated Lord He at

the moment, she wouldn't lie. Things were already delicate between the Zhang and Song empires, and Fen would not have unnecessary stress added to the situation. She still knew her duty to her family and people. "Aaron did speak up to the man, but with good reason."

"Oh?" The empress frowned and thought for a moment. "We'll send him away, quietly, to appease Lord He before he goes. I'll have Lady Hsin send someone else to finish—"

"No," Fen rushed, not wanting Aaron to go. The mere idea of possibly seeing him during the day was her whole reason for getting up. It was like a game she played with herself when with the suitors, a game to see if she could find him in the distance. Just one glimpse of him made her happy.

The empress waited, her expression blank.

"He did nothing... I mean, he did speak up, but he was defending me. And, well, he's very talented at what he does with the silks." Fen made a weak noise and stopped babbling.

"What is this man to you?" The empress didn't move.

Fen took a slow breath, hoping it wasn't obvious under her mother's probing gaze. "What do you mean?"

"What is this man to you?"

"He's...talented. I respect that talent and would hate to lose such a good designer."

"Mm-hmm." The empress stood. "A mother knows, Fen."

"There is nothing to know," she lied, instantly feeling bad about it.

"Make sure there isn't."

"He saved my life. I don't want him punished for that. If you are reading anything by my defense of him, it's gratitude. Besides, he's not like us. How could you think anything more? As you said, I have plenty of men to attend me."

"How could I ever punish a man for saving you?" The empress smiled, reaching out to touch her face lightly before pulling away. Her mother walked toward the door. "I'll speak to your father. He will know the perfect way to make Lord He's stay short without offending him. Lady Hsin's man will stay long enough to finish his task, but I think it would be best if you limit your exposure to him. It's all right to be grateful, but you don't want him getting the wrong impression. Men like him often do. Besides, with new suitors soon to join us, you'll be busy attending your guests."

"About that..." Fen said.

The empress paused in leaving, turning expectantly.

"I know you worry, but can't we call off the suitors? I don't wish to marry—not anyone. Please, don't make me do this." Fen's eyes met her mother's. "Do not force me to marry."

The empress sighed and sat back down, threading her hands in her lap. "I remember a story I heard when I was a very young girl. In the ancient times, back when our people were still on the planet Old Earth, long before other planets were known to humans, there was a lineage of emperors. After long wars, their military supply of horses was depleted."

"Horses?" Fen asked, trying to remember what they were. The word was vaguely familiar.

"They were animals, like the *yaoguai* only uglier, and used to carry things around on their backs," the Empress explained. *Yaoguai* were furry, bright red beasts of burden used by farmers and miners to pull carts. "I'm sure you've seen images. The old computer scans in the library show primitive pictures of them."

"And the military used them to haul what? Weapons?"

"To carry their warriors into battle. The main function was to haul humans around. The point is, the emperor needed these horses so badly and his country was so depleted that he sent men to raid a neighboring country filled with barbarians to steal them. But even then, he needed more. So, he traded a female from his house to the barbarian emperor he'd raided, in exchange for a thousand of the creatures."

"I don't understand," Fen said, confused.

"I do what I do for you, Fen, not a country. Be happy that your fate isn't dependent on the needs of the people. Whenever you feel life is rough here at the palace, or that your father and I expect too much in wanting to see you happily settled and safe within your homeland, remember that story. At least you are not being traded to a foreigner for horses. You still have a choice in who you marry. Times are not so bad. All we ask of you is to meet the suitors and consider them."

Fen managed a smile, though her mother hardly made her feel better with her little story. The empress was like that though. She just didn't see things the same way as her daughters.

At the empress' expectant look, Fen nodded. She couldn't crush her mother's hopeful expression. Not now. Weakly, she said, "Please give my excuses tonight at dinner. I think I might skip it." She touched her throat to emphasize her meaning.

The empress nodded, went back to the door and smiled as she said, "Lights."

The lights shut off, leaving Fen in the dark. She closed her eyes, hearing the empress shut her in her room.

"Fire and water." An's voice interrupted her rest.

"What?" Fen opened her eyes, but it was still dark.

"Fire and water. First the flames, then you nearly drown. Don't you think it odd?" An demanded.

"What do you mean?" Fen asked.

"Two elements, two attempts on your life."

"An, who would want to hurt me?" Fen dismissed. "You're just finally feeling guilty for messing with Captain Jarek's crew. That's why you're thinking of the elements."

An, in a fit of outrage, had predicted some of Princess Mei's friends and crewmen would have to find love by the five Lintianese elements—fire, earth, water, metal and wood. Last time Fen had talked to her sister, the men were still tormented by the prediction. An refused to clarify it or take it back. Unfortunately, none of them knew whether An's prediction was real or merely a means to mess with the poor humanoids.

"I don't feel guilty for putting that space trash in

their place," An denied. "Besides, this has nothing to do with your sister. This has to do with you."

"The railing on the bridge snapped. No one tried to kill me, unless you count Lord He just standing by and watching me drown."

"Did he push you?" An asked. "I told you not to bother with him."

"No," Fen denied. "It just broke. The bridge is old. I was just the unlucky one who discovered the weakness in the design."

"Too bad."

"Grandmother!" Fen sat up, absently saying, "Lights."

The lights turned on. An floated next to the bed, her arms crossed, her hair drifting as if the breeze stirred her transparent body. "I don't mean it like that. He's from the Singhai Empire."

"Don't warmonger. It's not—"

"I wouldn't dare," An interrupted. "But our warriors could well take the Song if there was to be a war. I can't believe your mother dared to invite Singhai nobles here. It's like she hoped you would pick one of them." An shivered in disgust.

"Two nobles from the borders," Fen corrected, "and she invited more Muntong than Singhai by far. The odds are in our side's favor."

An snorted, her look saying it didn't matter.

"You didn't get your offering today, did you?" Fen asked, understanding instantly what brought on An's bad mood.

"Your mother is disrespectful," An mumbled.

"You did trick her into thinking Mei would marry Prince Song Lok."

"I did no such thing. I said a foreign prince. Prince Jarek is both. She assumed Prince Lok." An snorted. "Like I'd let either of you girls marry a Song. Do you know how they treat their women in Singhai? You would be no better than a servant...worse, lower."

Fen thought of Lord He, and drawled wryly, "I can well imagine."

"Now, this Aaron," An said.

"Stop stirring trouble," Fen warned.

"I wasn't the one stirring," An laughed, a breeze swirling around her body, drifting her toward the door.

"Hey," Fen yelled. "Don't you dare spy on me, Grandmother."

The laughter grew, only to fade as An left the room.

"Ugh." Fen sighed, turning to hit her pillow. She was tired and didn't want to think. "Lights!"

Aaron's damp hair lifted in the breeze. He wished he'd been given more time to clean up before being summoned to the Hall of Infinite Wisdom. Emperor Zhang and the empress were there, waiting for him. He tried to tell himself that they only wanted to see him about saving Fen, or at worst about his insolence toward Lord He. But what if there was more? What if they knew what he'd done with their daughter? What he even now wanted to do again—consequences be damned. A night in Fen's arms would be worth a thousand deaths. Poetically, it sounded nice. In reality, he was frightened.

Bravery is acting through fear, he told himself as he steeled his nerves for what was to come.

He saw a few of the nobles walking along the

paths as he made his way. They didn't give him a second glance. The men's clothes were bright and of a fine quality, with delicate embroidery and trim. Aaron looked down at his own drab clothes. Sure, he did own a few good tunics, given that he oversaw so much at Lady Hsin's, but while at the palace, he wasn't allowed to wear the nicer clothing. If nobles saw him dressed in finery, they would no longer wish to have that same finery. If they no longer wished to have it, silk would stop selling as well and he'd be turned out from his job. That is why he now wore the dark brown, undecorated tunic and loose black breeches.

Still, it would have been nice to be dressed in a way befitting royal eyes—and not just any royal eyes, Fen's parents.

Why did he even dwell on it? Nothing could come of himself and the princess. At most they'd be lovers for the briefest of times. She would move on and he'd be left with the memories to drive him into old age. Already he could see himself an old man, drinking alone, torn and withered by the memory of a young butterfly from long ago.

The Hall of Infinite Wisdom was only one building within the palace walls, located in the center. It was an imposing sight, its dark red walls and yellow-tiled roofs matching the rest of the palace buildings. As he was led inside, he was given no time to collect himself. Two warrior god statues stood next to the gilded entryway, their life-size figures prepared for battle.

Torchlight added ambiance to the hall and wouldn't truly be needed until nightfall. Above, the outside sun was reflected in through small holes in the ceiling. They were so tiny and inlaid into the intricate design that it was impossible to see them.

Instantly, his eyes went to the high thrones. The emperor and empress sat above the hall on a plat form, surrounded by carved golden dragons that looked as if they coiled around them.

The emperor had a long mustache that hung down the front of his tunic, and both royal persons wore matching yellow embroidered silk decorated with imperial red dragons and ancient symbols. Just like when their people had lived on Old Earth long ago, red and gold were the colors of royalty, repre-senting fortune and wealth. The imperial couple's clothing matched the red and gold of the palace buildings.

His ears buzzed and he didn't hear as the servant announced him to the royal couple. It was unneces-sary, as he'd met with them already about the order of silk. The empress motioned the servant to leave and when they were alone in the large, unwelcoming hall, she ordered him to come forward. He did so respectfully, his head down, his eyes on the floor as he bowed low.

"We wish to convey our thanks in saving our daughter," the empress said. "Such assistance will not be forgotten."

"It was my honor to serve," Aaron answered.

There was silence, and he wondered why they didn't dismiss him. Then he felt as if someone had drawn near. He glanced forward, surprised to see the empress' feet so close. She'd come down off the platform. He looked up to see the emperor still sat in his palace, his face blank, his eyes forward.

"The princess would have thanked you herself," the empress said softly. "But she is busy recovering from her ordeal."

"If I might inquire, is she...? Will she be...?"

"Yes, she is fine," the empress said. "Thank you for your concern."

Relief washed over him. He hadn't realized he'd been so worried. Aaron caught himself smiling, not knowing when the look had crossed his face. He quickly wiped the expression off his features and waited.

"The princess is very grateful to you," the empress said. "She wishes me to convey her thoughts. You understand with so many suitors, and her so close to choosing a husband, that she cannot receive you herself to express her thanks."

The comment was cutting, but said in such a pleasant, serene way that he could hardly find fault in the empress for saying it. Nor could he argue when she continued.

"You've done well for us in your work and I'll be commending you to Lady Hsin. But, I must insist you do not go to the royal sleeping chambers again."

She knows. Aaron swallowed. *The empress knows I've slept with Fen.*

"It's a small matter this once, as you were merely delivering her to her chambers after her fall, but you took measurements the evening before without a chaperone, and we do not want her suitors discouraged by such innocence."

She doesn't know. Aaron bit the inside of his mouth, concentrating on not giving anything away with his expressions.

"Do you understand, Piers Aaron, why she must not thank you herself?" the empress asked.

Aaron wasn't fool enough to miss the woman's meaning. The empress didn't want him near her daughter. She didn't want him ruining Fen's chances at marriage—a chance Fen obviously wanted if her mother was to be believed. And none of the royal family wanted rumors started about the princess and a servant.

"*Shi*," he said, nodding in understanding. It might as well have been a direct order. He wasn't to go visit Fen in her chambers again. Any hope he had of being intimate with her died. He thought of their plan to meet by the weapons building. She'd already risked taking him in her room. He shouldn't let her risk herself yet again. There was no choice in the matter. He would go only to make sure she was safe, but he wouldn't let her see him.

Let her think he didn't want to meet her. Then she'd be done with him.

"You may go," the empress said. "I am sure you have much to do."

"*Shi*," Aaron agreed, bowing. "Thank you, Empress."

FEN PACED HER CHAMBERS. Two days since she'd been saved, and not once did Aaron come to see how she was. It was bad enough he'd stood her up outside the weapons building. She'd waited for him, looking all around, before realizing they never really set a time. It was late in the morning when she finally gave up and went to bed.

The missed rendezvous was disappointing, but she could make excuses for his absence. However, it didn't excuse the fact that he hadn't found a way to get into her company after that. It wouldn't have been hard for him to come up with a justification. He could have delivered material samples, brought her partial gowns for fittings, lost part of her order. If she could come up with so many reasons, then why couldn't he? The least he could do is come and check on her.

What was worse, she hadn't seen him around the palace grounds at all.

Lord He took his leave the day after her accident. His young friend, Lord Gao, went with him. Fen wasn't sure what her father had said, but they parted on decent terms. Both sides obviously knew what had happened to Fen facilitated the departure, but no one was speaking of it. Such was the way of politics.

Since she was deemed well enough to leave her bed, she'd spent an afternoon walking with Tan Ho. The man didn't speak much, and when he did, his voice was so soft Fen could barely hear him. Then, she had tea with Fei Bin, though she couldn't remember a thing he said. An had been speaking above him the whole time, poking fun at the man's imperfections. Fen threatened to take away her offerings if she ever did that again.

Chu Dun, Chi Tan, and Mou Tian took her on a picnic in the imperial gardens. All she could think of the whole time was how An claimed Mou Tian had been self-pleasuring himself too much. Then, when she saw his eyes light up as Haun joined them, she knew that Mou Tian was definitely not pleasuring himself to thoughts of her.

Ruan Ping was supposed to spend time with her, but his mother beckoned him home and he left before much could be made of their courtship. Fen couldn't say she was disappointed. She had enough men to keep her busy for a lifetime.

Deng Li from Changshangu serenaded her with song. He had a great voice, and afterward they had talked for nearly two hours. She found him to be pleasant and by far the most likable man she'd been courted by. Out of all her suitors, she got along with him and Ye Shing the best. Shing's brother didn't spcak much and never asserted himself toward her. She assumed Ye Yuan wasn't very interested.

But throughout the whole ordeal, there was one man she thought about constantly. Piers Aaron. Why didn't he come for her? She had been extremely clear that she wanted him to. The nights after her accident, she waited for him in her bed, willing him to come to her—her body hot and ready until even the slightest movement made her squirm in arousal. If not for An making an offhanded comment about him, she'd have thought he'd left the palace without saying goodbye.

More than slightly irritated and needing to relax after days of being courted, Fen grabbed a black silk robe and slid it on to hide the brighter color of her nightclothes. Slipping out of her chambers, she tiptoed quietly down the hall and out the front door. It was late, and with all the ancestors they had around there was no need for palace guards—of course, only the royal family knew that.

Péng You Hall was the next building over and it didn't take her long to run barefoot down the path. Hiding along the wall, she closed her eyes. She'd come this far, only she didn't know what room he was in.

Closing her eyes, Fen said dolefully, "Grandmother? Zhang An, are you there? I need you."

The spirit instantly appeared. "What are you waiting for? I have a bet going that you'll make it all the way inside."

"You're watching me?" Fen gasped, feeling violated.

"Oh, no, no, we don't watch that." An grinned, as if reading her mind. "And not everyone knows, just a few of us. Don't worry, we don't interfere."

"Mm-hmm," Fen hummed dryly in disbelief.

"Are you nervous?" An asked.

"No, I..." Fen hesitated, but her desire to be with him was greater than her apprehension of An knowing she was going. "He saved my life and then didn't come to see if I was all right afterward. It's very

CHELLE M. PILLOW

ghtclothes. Slipping out of her chambers, she
toed quietly down the hall and out the front door.
was late, and with all the ancestors they had
ound there was no need for palace guards—of
urse, only the royal family knew that.

Péng You Hall was the next building over and it
dn't take her long to run barefoot down the path.
iding along the wall, she closed her eyes. She'd
me this far, only she didn't know what room he
as in.

Closing her eyes, Fen said dolefully, "Grand-
other? Zhang An, are you there? I need you."

The spirit instantly appeared. "What are you
aiting for? I have a bet going that you'll make it all
e way inside."

"You're watching me?" Fen gasped, feeling
iolated.

"Oh, no, no, we don't watch that." An grinned, as
reading her mind. "And not everyone knows, just a
ew of us. Don't worry, we don't interfere."

"Mm-hmm," Fen hummed dryly in disbelief.

"Are you nervous?" An asked.

"No, I..." Fen hesitated, but her desire to be with
im was greater than her apprehension of An
nowing she was going. "He saved my life and then
idn't come to see if I was all right afterward. It's very

Fen paced her chambers. Two days since she'd
been saved, and not once did Aaron come to see how
she was. It was bad enough he'd stood her up outside
the weapons building. She'd waited for him, looking
all around, before realizing they never really set a
time. It was late in the morning when she finally gave
up and went to bed.

The missed rendezvous was disappointing, but
she could make excuses for his absence. However, it
didn't excuse the fact that he hadn't found a way to
get into her company after that. It wouldn't have
been hard for him to come up with a justification. He
could have delivered material samples, brought her
partial gowns for fittings, lost part of her order. If she
could come up with so many reasons, then why

couldn't he? The least he could do is come and check on her.

What was worse, she hadn't seen him around the palace grounds at all.

Lord He took his leave the day after her accident. His young friend, Lord Gao, went with him. Fen wasn't sure what her father had said, but they parted on decent terms. Both sides obviously knew what had happened to Fen facilitated the departure, but no one was speaking of it. Such was the way of politics.

Since she was deemed well enough to leave her bed, she'd spent an afternoon walking with Tan Ho. The man didn't speak much, and when he did, his voice was so soft Fen could barely hear him. Then, she had tea with Fei Bin, though she couldn't remember a thing he said. An had been speaking above him the whole time, poking fun at the man's imperfections. Fen threatened to take away her offerings if she ever did that again.

Chu Dun, Chi Tan, and Mou Tian took her on a picnic in the imperial gardens. All she could think of the whole time was how An claimed Mou Tian had been self-pleasuring himself too much. Then, when she saw his eyes light up as Haun joined them, she knew that Mou Tian was definitely not pleasuring himself to thoughts of her.

Ruan Ping was supposed to spend ti
but his mother beckoned him home
before much could be made of their co
couldn't say she was disappointed. She
men to keep her busy for a lifetime.

Deng Li from Changshangu serenad
song. He had a great voice, and afterwa
talked for nearly two hours. She found
pleasant and by far the most likable man
courted by. Out of all her suitors, she got
him and Ye Shing the best. Shing's bro
speak much and never asserted himself t
She assumed Ye Yuan wasn't very intereste

But throughout the whole ordeal, the
man she thought about constantly. Piers A
didn't he come for her? She had been extre
that she wanted him to. The nights afte
dent, she waited for him in her bed, willi
come to her—her body hot and ready unti
slightest movement made her squirm in
not for An making an offhanded comment
she'd have thought he'd left the palace with
goodbye.

More than slightly irritated and needin
after days of being courted, Fen grabbed a
robe and slid it on to hide the brighter col

irresponsible of him, and I'm going to... I'm going to...to..."

An lifted a ghostly brow.

"I'm going to yell at him."

"Ah, sure you are." An laughed. "So, what's stopping you?"

"I don't know where he's staying. You've been in there; which room is his?"

An's smile widened.

"Grandmother?" Fen insisted.

"Third door on the left," An said. "Have fun."

"Stay out of the room," Fen warned as the woman disappeared. "And nothing is going to happen."

Péng You Hall was less decorated than the royal chambers, but it was still beautifully done. The decoration was simple, with two stone figures guarding the doors, their arms crossed, their eyes wide open as if seeing everything. Unlike the other statues, these two had small smiles carved into their welcoming faces.

Inside was a foyer, with a serene fountain. Its running water added a tranquility to the room. Leading away from the foyer were three halls of guest rooms. Each guest room was different in décor, but all were modeled after Old Earth. The halls had old rock carvings spaced between the thick doors. They were old religious figures once found in caves. Fen loved them. Even now they resonated an old power. It awed her to think of what these statues had seen—what planets, what lands and people. How many of her kind had touched them, prayed, worshiped and hoped?

Going down the hall to her left, she hoped An wouldn't trick her. Now that she was here, she was nervous. This wasn't exactly smart of her. What if he wasn't there? What if another suitor saw her in here? What if Aaron turned her away?

Her palm flat, she lightly tapped on his door. If he didn't answer, she'd turn and leave.

Not really giving him enough noise to hear, she pulled back.

Okay, that settles it. He's not here.

She moved to go, cowardice taking over her as her mind swam with doubts.

The door opened, and a perplexed Aaron shoved his head out in question. His eyes met hers and she instantly went still. Fen couldn't breathe. She'd somehow forgotten how his eyes impacted her with their deep intensity. One look and she felt as if he strangled her soul, holding it captive. She wanted him to have it.

All anger and doubt left her. This is where she wanted to be. When she looked at him, she didn't care about her parents, about the suitors, about their stations in life. Honor and duty paled to his face, to the promise of his arms.

Finally, he drew his eyes away, forcing them down as he opened the door completely. His voice soft, as if mindful of the other rooms, he said, "Princess. There was no need for you to come here. I'll gladly have a servant deliver your gowns to you."

Fen glanced back and forth down the hall. Seeing it was empty, she pushed her hand into Aaron's chest and made him step back into his room so she could enter. He wore the drab browns she always saw him in. The material molded to his chest, revealing what she already knew to be a fine span of muscles.

She quietly closed the door behind her. The chambers were a dark green, from the soft, cashmere rugs to the old tapestries showing two-dimensional people in battle. Fen instantly noticed a figure of a warrior sitting astride an animal. A horse, undoubtedly. A scroll or text, blessing the occupant and welcoming him to the palace, hung on a wall. The parchment was weathered, but the writing as bold as the day it was done. Decorative pillows were on the bed, showing a scene of a bride being led away by a procession of servants.

"Princess," Aaron said.

Before he could continue, she lifted her hand. "You haven't come to me. Why? Did you even try to meet me by the weapons building?"

"It is not my place to—"

"You should have come. I waited for you to come." Her hands shook. Nothing she'd thought of telling him would come out. "Why did you stay away? Did you not wish to be with me again?"

"You have suitors. You're to be married. I'm just a servant. To be seen with me would—"

"Don't say that," Fen demanded, not wishing to hear the truth. If he told her they couldn't be, it would crush the little hope she did carry. She knew they couldn't be together, not beyond anything physical. Her parents wouldn't allow it.

At least Mei had married a prince. And Jin's wife was a special case, as her sole knowledge of the ancient form of Wushu made her valuable to the family. But Fen was the only daughter left, and Aaron had nothing the family could not get elsewhere.

She began to pace, shaking her head. "What is it about you? Why can't I stop thinking of you? I walk the gardens and I wish it was you with me, not Tan Ho. When I pour tea, I wish to pour it for you. When I hear Chu Dun laugh or Chi Tan speak, I long for it to be your laughter, your voice. I watch for you in the distance, I wait all day to see you looking at me, and you never come. Why don't you come to me? How can I feel this, and yet you can stay away?"

His mouth opened, but he didn't speak.

"Why don't you say anything to me? You just look at me, and I feel you want to say something. I feel you want to and yet you say nothing, do nothing but stand there. Why, Aaron?"

Visibly swallowing, he lifted his chin. His tone hard, he asked, "How do you know to sense these things? Perhaps you are just nervous about marriage and imagine that which is not there."

"Stop." Fen shook her head, laughing though the sound was hardly pleasant. "You cannot fool me with those words. I have gifts, Aaron, the gift of knowing others. It's not just a sense, it's a power. The Jade Phoenix blessed me, as it does all royal children, at my birth. I know you want me. It's like a little thread that joins us, delicate and fine. I can feel you tugging at it, pulling me closer."

"I've never heard of this power," he said, his face ever serious.

"You shouldn't be hearing of it now." Fen took a deep breath. What was it about him? She trusted him; trusted him enough to reveal family secrets without thought. "It's a private ceremony, one we do not tell the Lintianese people about for fear that someone might try to take the Jade Phoenix for themselves. If that happened, the power of the Phoenix would be spread out too thin and no one would benefit."

"If this is not to be known, why do you tell me now?"

Did his face have to be so blank? She could feel the emotions raging inside him, confusing her own. The feelings were stronger as each day passed, as she learned to feel them, to trust herself to feel them. Why didn't he let her see the emotion on his handsome face? Why couldn't he let her in?

"I can't seem to keep my mouth shut when I'm with you," Fen admitted. "I'm near you and I want to start confessing every thought in my head."

"Then perhaps you should go." He made a move toward the door. "I don't want you to say anything that you'll regret later."

"I don't want to go." Fen refused to move as she stood, staring at him. "Quit trying to get rid of me."

Unhurriedly, she pulled off her belt, opening the

black robe. Her nightclothes were short, designed for hot nights. Though outside was cool, she couldn't think of a hotter night than what she was experiencing right now. The thin material clung to her as she pushed the robe off her shoulders. She felt the red silk rubbing along her breasts, catching slightly on her erect nipples. Beneath the silk she was naked, and the knowledge made her flesh tingle.

"Do you really want me to leave, Aaron? Do you want me never to bother you again?"

Before his mouth even opened, she sensed that he was going to lie and say yes.

"*Shi,*" he said.

"Liar," she accused, going toward him. He didn't stop her as she took his face in her hands. "Liar."

Fen kissed him, bringing his mouth to hers. It was bittersweet, the ache she felt deep inside. Every part of her wanted to be here, but she knew she shouldn't. She wished he'd take over, make the first move, say what she felt he wanted.

Fen slipped her tongue along his lips, forcing them to part. Two hesitant hands touched her hips. She pressed her body closer to his, settling along his hard length. Moaning softly, she turned her head to the side, opening her mouth, prompting him to kiss her deep and hard. He did kiss her, but there was still restraint in him, as if he was unwilling to turn all of himself over to her.

Even as she hated it, she understood why he held back. Desperation made her press harder, sawing her mouth against his, trying to break through the last bit of his control.

It didn't work. Aaron wouldn't turn himself over completely.

Frustrated, she pulled away, making distance between her heated body and his. Breathing hard, she demanded, "Tell me you want me."

Aaron glanced down his body, to the obvious protrusion that answered her question.

Fen lifted her hands, running them over the red silk of her short gown. She let the material lift, giving the barest peek of her upper thighs before letting it fall once more. Her palms skimmed her nipples, sending jolts of awareness over her skin. The erotic sensation centered in her stomach. She wanted him so badly, was crazy with desire and need.

"Tell me you want me," Fen repeated. His silent answer wasn't good enough. She needed to hear him say it.

"*Shi,*" he said, nodding.

Fen gave him a slow smile. Lifting her hand to

her shoulder, she toyed with the thin strap. "I *said*, tell me you want me."

"I want you."

The words were soft but unmistakable. Pleasure erupted within her at his admission. She felt how hard it was for him to say the words, but she was glad he did. As a woman, she needed to hear them.

"And I you," she answered, just as softly.

Aaron moved forward, pulling her into his arms. He kissed her, running his tongue along her lips before moving to her throat. Teeth grazed her skin, biting lightly. Fen shivered, gasping at the rough, animalistic way he touched her. His hands ran over her sides, pulling up her gown as he caressed her through the silk. They were so strong, gripping her tight. He kneaded her flesh, pulling her tight against his arousal.

"You are so soft, like the wings of a butterfly." Even as he said it, he bit her neck in heavy kisses. "I'm scared I'll crush you."

"And you're solid as a rock," she answered, touching his biceps. "Butterflies land on rocks all the time and come away unharmed."

He groaned a response, but she couldn't under-stand the words. His arms swept beneath her, lifting her easily as he carried her toward his bed. Fen touched his face, holding it as she kissed him. His name left her lips on a moan. Being with him felt so right, so perfect, she couldn't imagine being any place else. He laid her on the soft mattress. His hands swept down over her, brushing warmth along the silk.

"I want you, Aaron," she said. "I want your strong hands on me. I love your hands."

With his lids heavy over his eyes, he crawled down her body. Starting at her feet, he massaged his way up her calf to her knee, only to move to the other side. She jolted when he touched the other foot, giggling as the soft touch tickled her flesh. Instantly, his caress became harder, the rough texture and strong grip like magic to her skin. It was a strange blend of hard and soft, gentle and forceful. Fen moaned. He massaged up her thighs, pushing the silk up as he worked.

She watched in the brighter light of the room. "Lights dim. Fire."

Aaron stopped, looking up in surprise as the palace mainframe listened to her.

"They were installed a few years ago," Fen said, liking the soft, seductive glow against his skin. She parted her legs, hoping he'd be enticed to move higher, slipping right into her aching body.

Aaron did move up, but slid over her hips, skipping her middle. He rubbed her arms and hands before pulling her to sitting so he could pull her nightclothes off completely. Fen squirmed, panting as he circled her breasts, gently skimming the nipples.

Aaron groaned in response. She knew he was aroused, could see his erection pressing against his pants. His eyes lit in hazy pleasure, heating intensely as he watched his hands on her breasts. As he worked his way down, he straddled her thighs.

"Take off your shirt," she ordered, longing to see him, to touch him. Fen reached for his chest, inching the material up as she explored his body through the brown tunic. He tossed the shirt aside, instantly moving back to her flesh. "I love looking at your chest."

Fen wished he'd speak, but each time it seemed he was going to, he held back. The massage was wonderful, kindling the ache within her, but she wanted more. She wanted the wildly passionate, rough man who'd taken her like a commoner.

"Don't treat me like a princess," Fen said. "I don't have to be a princess right now."

He glanced at her and an emotion filtered through his gaze.

"What?" she asked, needing to know what he

was feeling. She'd felt the strangeness in him before, the first time they'd come together.

"You act as if we are a different species. First you say to me, 'Take me as you would one of your women,' and now you ask that I do not treat you like a princess." He rubbed her chest, but not with the intensity of before.

"Not different species," Fen said, "but different people."

"You mean to say class." Aaron shook his head.

"Well..." Fen hesitated, but he was right. That is what she meant. "Yes. We come from different backgrounds."

"And you think that my kind is so different from those who are rich?"

"I really hope so," Fen answered honestly. "I'm tired of men who don't say what they mean, only take what they want without thinking of others. They lack fire and passion...the fire and passion I feel inside of you, the fire and passion I feel inside myself when I am near you. I'm tired of men treating me as if I'm some delicate flower. I don't need poetry recited to me. I don't *want* poetry."

"But what if poetry is inspired by your beauty?" His caresses became bolder. "What if, when I look at you, I see a delicate butterfly, so light and fragile and graceful, she should be floating above mere mortals like me? What if I've always seen that when I look at you?"

"Always? You say that as if you've seen me your whole life." Fen bit her lips, moaning softly as his hands grazed across her chest. With each pass, his touch became harder, rougher, just as she liked him to be.

"In parades," he admitted, "and when you came to the factory at Lady Hsin's. But you never saw me. How could you? Me, in the crowd of so many eyes."

Fen gasped, suddenly remembering where she'd seen him before. "I did see you at Lady Hsin's."

"You lie to appease my vanity." There were no accusations in the words, but Fen felt the hint of truth in them—truth as he believed it to be.

"No, it was nearly ten years ago. You were carrying silk in the factory while Lady Hsin took me to see her butterflies. The light was dim and we bumped into you. I didn't see the blue of your eyes. That is why I didn't recognize you right away. Your eyes threw my memory of it. But you are the one who designed the yellow silk I bought nearly ten years ago. I loved that silk. It was the only time I liked a fabric that was designed by someone other than Lady Hsin."

He gave a short laugh. His hands renewed their journey at her neck, sliding between her breasts to her stomach. He touched her hips, her sides, working his way toward her sex.

"What?" Fen asked, parting her thighs. It was hard with him straddling her.

"I..."

"What?"

"I design all the fabrics, but Lady Hsin does not like people to know she no longer has a hand in her business. She is too busy entertaining guests." He moaned, leaning over to suck a nipple between his lips. The other breast received the same treatment from his hand, pinching and caressing. The sudden caress caused a shock to run over her, coursing a wayward path over her limbs, centering in the heated core of her sex.

Finding a strength she didn't know she had, she pushed his chest, knocking him to the side so she could climb on top of him. "You betray your employer. I shall have to punish you for that."

He grinned, not at all concerned by her sultry threat. She was glad. It meant he was starting to relax around her, trust her.

Fen wiggled against his arousal, rubbing her sex against him through his pants. She explored his chest, discovering every peak and valley, pinching his nipples as he did the same to her.

"I can't wait," Fen said, desperately reaching to free his cock. She pulled at his waistband, moving it down just enough to let his distended flesh spring up. With his pants still on, she grabbed him, stroking the smooth length of his shaft before lifting up to bring it to her moist opening.

She lowered herself down, taking him deep and fast.

Aaron gasped, his mouth opening wide as he arched beneath her. Raking her nails against his chest, she bucked her hips hard. He took her hips in hand, lifting and pulling as he pushed into her. The desperate pace was just want she needed.

Aaron sat up part way, leaning her body back so that his shaft bent forward. The hard muscles of his stomach strained to hold the position. Fen put her hands back on his legs. The new position rubbed his cock along the sweet spot hidden in her depths, asserting pressure and making her instantly start to quiver.

"Ah, *shi*," he urged, slipping a finger to encircle her clit. "Come for me."

Fen jerked hard, orgasming at the intense plea-sure. Aaron grunted, as if taking his orgasm into himself. When she started to come down, she realized that was exactly what he did.

His cock still hard, he pulled her off of it.

"You do not wish to be treated as a delicate princess," he said, breathing heavily. "Then I shall not treat you as such."

The words were enough to cause a renewal of arousal to stir within her.

"Crawl down my body and take me into your mouth," he ordered. "Let me watch you suck me."

Fen pulled his pants from his legs, leaving his body as naked as hers. Putting her knees between his, she pushed his thighs open and leaned over, taking his shaft into her mouth. The taste of her body mingled with the slightly salty taste of his flesh. She moaned.

"Ah, that's right," Aaron said in breathless approval. "Lick your cream all off me."

Fen sucked harder, taking him as deep as she could.

Suddenly, he pulled her off and flung her on her back. His body was instantly on hers, pressing inside her once more. Hooking her knee with his arm, he lifted her leg. In that moment, nothing mattered. She felt like a woman with Aaron—a real woman.

They climaxed in unison. As Aaron came, he

pulled out, releasing his seed onto the bed. Fen was too tired to move. Her bones felt as if they'd melted and every nerve was numb and relaxed. Aaron grabbed a corner of the blanket and lifted it over their bodies before holding her close. For a long time, they didn't speak, merely held each other as the crackle of fire serenaded them with its peaceful song.

Fen cuddled in Aaron's arms. She was tired, but she didn't want to fall asleep and miss a second of her time with him. Skating a finger along his chest, she sighed, "I haven't been this relaxed since I was allowed to plant the imperial gardens."

"You planted the gardens?" he asked, leaning back to better study her face.

"Well, not me, but I designed it and oversaw the workers." Fen chuckled. "Okay, so I did plant a few of the bushes when no one was looking. I even got a scar from it."

"Oh, yeah?" He lifted his arm to better look at her naked body. "Where?"

Fen giggled, feeling giddy as she lifted her leg out from beneath the blanket. Pointing at her inner knee, she showed him a tiny line scar. It was barely noticeable.

"Looks life threatening," he teased.

Fen was shocked. Did he just make a joke?

Pushing up, Aaron leaned over and kissed it. A shiver worked over her and she touched his head.

"I..." Fen stopped herself just as he was about to confess feelings she had yet to analyze.

He nodded. "I know."

"You do?" She held her breath, looking deep into his blue eyes.

"*Shi,* you have to go," he said. "I know you cannot be caught with me."

That wasn't what she'd been about to say, but she let him believe that. "*Shi,* I must leave."

Fen got out of bed and picked up her black robe off the floor. Without bothering to put her night-clothes back on, she slipped the robe over her body and knotted the belt. Holding her red gown, she turned to him. His eyes were heated and he hadn't moved.

"I want to see you again," she said.

"You will."

"When?" Fen took a step toward the door.

"Whenever you wish, Princess."

The title was like a slap in the face. She wasn't sure if that was how he meant it, but it effectively reminded her of the gap between them. During sex, they might be able to pretend, but when she walked out that door, duty called.

"A PEASANT. She gives her royal body to an undeserving peasant!"

Anger burned within the man's soul. Each time he closed his eyes he could still hear them together, the soft sounds of their passion through the unworthy servant's door. It was bad enough they were housed in the same building as the man, but *this*? How could Princess Fen let that man touch her? Aaron wasn't worthy of her.

He gripped the base of one of the old statues that lined the halls of Péng You Hall. His heart beating hard in his chest, he felt as if he couldn't breathe. A glimmer appeared near him and he looked at the transparent figure with relief and fear. The woman was older, though her spirit form made her look young. She reached out, glancing her ghostly fingers over his head as if to comfort him.

"What do you ask of me?" the specter asked in the calm voice that always managed to set him at ease.

"Blessed ancestor, please, make her worthy for me once more. Purge her of this sin, strike it out of her like a metal blade to her cheating heart. Please, I beg you, purge her of this sin. Make her worthy. Make her worthy."

"And the unworthy man who dared touch her?" the spirit asked in a voice much calmer than his.

"I'll take care of him."

The figure didn't answer as it disappeared. Calming himself, he lifted his jaw and slowly made his way back to his own room.

15

FEN SMILED AT HER BROTHERS, happy to be spending time with them. They walked along the decorative pathways, aimless in direction, but together. Shen and Lian were at her sides, Haun a couple paces behind them. Fen really missed Mei and Jin, wishing that they were back home like before their marriages.

Another suitor had gone unexpectedly. Mou Tian was very sweet before he left, wishing her luck with her future decision. It was clear he'd only been there out of family duty.

"The other suitors have started to arrive," Shen said, grinning in brotherly mischief. "I sense some of them about to approach the palace gate."

Fen groaned. "Why'd you have to tell me that?"

"Because it's funny," Lian teased.

"Ha. Ha. Ha." Fen's tone was dry. "Hilarious."

"Remember all those years you and Mei giggled about our required attendance at the *Qi-zi* ceremony," Haun said. His tone was wistful, and Fen knew he missed Mei as much as she did. Haun and Mei had always had a special connection. Since Haun was the oldest and Mei the baby of the family, he'd always been protective of her and she'd always idolized him. "You thought it was so funny that we had to stand there looking at woman after woman for hours on end. Like a man could ever choose a bride out of that lineup."

"Jin did," Fen said.

"Ah, but he didn't, not really," Lian debated. "Francesca wasn't there as a bride. She was there to steal from us."

"Ugh, I hate this courtship thing. Why couldn't I just be left alone to decide my own fate? Or at least get possessed by an ancestor against my will like Jin." Fen rubbed the back of her neck. It was a beautiful day and she was with her family. She should not be so stressed. "Maybe if I'm lucky they'll all be like Mou Tian."

"And leave?" Shen questioned.

"And prefer Haun to me," Fen answered, giggling. She glanced back at him, winking audaciously. Haun's expression fell and he looked toward the front gate of the palace before turning back to her.

"Oh yeah," Fen confirmed, turning back to watch where she was going. "Most definitely."

"Lord Ye's son is an odd one," Shen said thoughtfully.

"Shing?" Fen asked.

"No, the other, Yuan." Shen motioned to his siblings that they should turn down the path. They followed without question. "He's very..."

"Clouded," Lian supplied.

"I'd call it odd," Haun said.

"I don't think he wants to be here," Fen said. "He never approaches me, and he seems little interested in being a suitor. I think he's bored."

"Shing approaches you often enough," Haun said. "You've spent more time with him than the others."

"Have I?" Fen asked, pretending like she didn't notice. Shing was the most assertive, putting himself out there. Since she didn't really care either way which one she was forced to spend time with, she just let him assert himself. He was charming and nice, a perfect gentleman.

Fen had discovered that she really didn't want a perfect gentleman. She wanted someone a little wilder, someone who knew the true meaning of desire and passion. Someone not afraid of hard work —especially in the bedroom.

"*Shi.*" Haun nodded.

"I think Deng Li would make a fine husband for you," Lian said. "He speaks very highly of you."

"You've talked to him?" Fen wasn't surprised that they were all keeping their eye on her.

"We've spoken to them all," Shen said.

"What did you say?" Fen stopped walking.

"That you are exceedingly self-centered," Haun said, pushing her from behind to get her going again.

"And *wanquan yuchun*," Lian added. "Very, very stupid."

"Vain," Shen said. "Ignorant."

"You flatter me," Fen said sarcastically, kicking a stone upon the path. Watching it roll, she thought of Aaron, longing to see him. She looked around, but he wasn't there.

"Lighten up," Shen teased, nudging her with his arm so she was thrown off balance as they walked.

She stumbled into Lian. He knocked her back

playfully and said, "We thought you didn't want them to like you."

"Well, I don't..." Fen frowned. Shen bumped her again, sending her back toward Lian. As Lian went to nudge her, she stepped back. He stumbled into Shen.

"So, you do want them to like you?" Haun asked, again pushing her to walk as he nudged her from behind.

"No," Fen denied quickly. "But I don't want to ruin my reputation or the reputation of the family."

"I sense," Lian said quietly, pausing to take a deep breath. "I sense that Fen likes someone."

"What?" Fen shook her head in denial.

"And she doesn't want to tell us about it," he continued.

"No," Fen said, guiltily thinking of Aaron. She couldn't tell them of him. "There is no one."

"Hmm," Haun said. "Definitely someone. I say Ye Shing."

"I say Deng Li," Lian said.

"I say Lord Ye," Shen laughed teasingly. "He is very enamored with you. He can barely keep his eyes off you when you are near him."

"Ugh, I think he'd be happy so long as I chose someone from his family." Fen shook her head. "You should hear him go on about his home. It's annoying."

"Ho!" a shout sounded.

Fen realized they'd come near the exercise grounds. The soldiers were throwing long spears. She stopped to watch.

"They haven't done that in a long while," she said, watching as the weapons arched high only to land with their metal tips in the ground. Most of the spears stood up from the ground, but a few fell over.

"The general asked permission this morning to revive some of the old fighting techniques to help the guards remember their usage. He said he was compelled to do a block of ancient training." Haun paused as the spears again flew through the air. The breeze picked up some, carrying them a little farther than before. The field was still a little bit away and Fen wanted to get closer to see. Haun, as if sharing her desire, started walking toward the field. As the spears landed, more falling over, he said, "It looks like the general was right. The men do need the practice."

"Let's watch," Fen said. Gardeners blocked the path up ahead. They were snipping flowers with long sheers and cutting back overgrowth in the shrubs. "Come on."

Fen started to thread her arm through Shen's

when she tripped. She let out a small sound of surprise as she fell.

Shen sprang into action, catching her arm. Lian was there a second later, pulling her other arm. They caught Fen's body, holding her a couple inches from impact with the ground. A sharp pain entered her chest and she gasped, glancing down. Shen and Lian pulled her arms, lifting her up. As she was righted on her feet, the light showed her what had hit her skin.

It was a piece of metal, and it stuck out of her left breast. Blood trickled down her bodice.

"Fen?" Shen asked, seeing it first.

"*Tianna,*" Lian swore.

Haun was there a second later. "Don't move her."

"What is it?" Lian asked.

"It looks like a piece of old metal. Maybe from a sedan?" Haun carefully examined the wound.

Fen closed her eyes. She didn't care where it came from, she just wanted it out of her. It really stung.

"Take a breath and hold it."

Fen did. Haun placed a hand on her shoulder as her two other brothers held her arms. The metal was pulled free and Haun instantly pushed his finger against the wound. It throbbed painfully, but she knew she'd live.

"A sedan?" Fen said, feeling woozy as she opened her eyes to look at the metal. "The last sedan used was to cart Francesca and it wasn't on this path. What's it doing here?"

"I don't know." Haun motioned Shen aside so he could lift her in his arms. Cradling her to his chest, Haun walked carefully toward the royal sleeping chambers. "Try not to move. We need to get you to the physician."

Shen's finger replaced Haun's on the wound.

"Metal."

Fen looked up, seeing An.

"Another element, and by your heart, no less," An continued. "I'm telling you. There is something to these attacks."

"It's not a sign," Fen answered. Her chest really hurt.

"A sign of what?" Lian looked up. Fen wasn't sure if he could see An or not.

"Grandmother An thinks I'm under attack," Fen admitted.

"What?" Shen and Haun said in unison.

"Why didn't you say something?" Lian asked.

"Under attack by whom?" Haun demanded, quickening his pace as he carried her over the pathway.

Fen wanted to tell him that she'd be all right, that she could walk, but her legs were shaking. Even she had to admit that the elements theory was starting to look real. "We're not sure. She thinks they're using the elements."

"The fire," Lian said, "in your room."

"*Shi.*" She bit her lip as they jolted her wound.

"And nearly drowning," Shen added. "Now metal."

"*Shi,*" she answered again.

"If it's true, that means whoever is responsible is using some sort of magical or supernatural means to make his attacks happen. And it means he only has two more elements to go. Wood and earth." Haun quickened his pace, calling out to the gardeners they passed to go get the physician at once. They instantly obeyed the order.

"Both hard to avoid," Lian said.

"Finally, you listen to reason," An said above them. All three brothers looked up, signifying they heard her words. "You must convince the emperor to take Fen out of the palace. She is not safe here. She needs to be hidden away for a while."

"Where should we go?" Haun asked.

"To Jin," An said. "Away from the suitors."

"Surely you're not suggesting a suitor had something to do with this?" Haun asked.

"I don't know who," An said. "If I did, we'd not be having this discussion. All I can say is that it's been getting colder here in the palace."

"What about the silk man? Piers?" Lian asked.

Fen had been concentrating on not crying out. Her eyes widened. There was no way Aaron would do this to her. Would he? She didn't want to believe it.

"He was conveniently nearby to save her," Lian said.

"Why does it have to be Aaron? Because he's not noble?" Fen demanded. "And why would he save me if he wanted to harm me?"

"Has anyone threatened you?" Haun asked, studying her carefully.

She shook her head in denial.

"I think it's that Lord Ye. He's an odd one," An said.

"Do you know something?" Haun asked.

An shook her head in denial.

"Then don't make conclusions about that which you don't know," Haun ordered her. "We can't go accusing anyone without proof."

An gasped, huffing in anger at his gruff tone. The

breeze stirred and she dissipated into the air, her body blowing away.

Fen coughed, closing her eyes as she rested her head against her brother's shoulder.

"The emperor will decide what is best," Haun said. "Let's just concentrate on getting you mended."

16

"Leave us."

Fen glanced up to see her father standing in her doorway. He tugged at his long mustache, something he did when he was agitated. Her brothers didn't move, but the physician instantly obeyed. Lian and Shen sat on the end of her bed. Haun stood next to her side.

"She's fine," Haun said. "Shen and Lian caught her before the scrap metal could pierce her heart."

"I've been told," the emperor said, his tone softening some. "And I am happy to see you well, daughter."

"What is it?" Fen asked, a sick feeling in her stomach.

"Leave us," the emperor said to his sons.

"Fen's well-being concerns all of us," Haun said.

"And this does not." The emperor frowned.

Haun placed fist to palm and bowed. Fen started to reach out to him to stop him from going. All three of her brothers left the room.

The emperor looked at her for a long time once they were alone. Fen couldn't meet his eye. Though they lived in the same palace, it was rare that they spoke. Her father was a busy man, a distant figure in her life. She loved him, respected him, would serve him and her family, but she didn't feel close to him as she imagined most daughters felt toward their fathers. Perhaps it was the price of being daughter to an emperor.

"Are you well?" he asked, motioning toward her chest where she was stabbed.

"*Shi.*"

"Zhang An has told me of her thoughts. She believes you are being attacked and bids me to send you to visit Jin in the countryside."

"She has said the same to me."

"Do you feel the same as she does? Do you feel you are being attacked?"

"It's hard to say." Fen motioned lightly to the side. She honestly didn't know.

"You've had no threats." It was more of a statement than a question. "I will post guards outside these walls at night and have asked our ancestors to watch over you. I can think of no safer place for you than within the palace walls, near family and guards. Besides, we have guests that are anxious for your company. For now, you will stay here."

Fen made a weak noise of disgust, unable to help herself.

"Hmm," the emperor grunted thoughtfully. "The empress tells me that you seem to be taking a liking to Ye Shing."

Fen wasn't sure how to answer, so said nothing.

"Deng Li?" the emperor asked, not moving from his place by the door. He looked as uncomfortable in her room as she was having him there. Her father never visited her there, not since she was a very little girl about to be reprimanded for picking all the flowers in the garden and laying them on the path-ways. It wasn't bad, except she'd done it the day before visiting dignitaries from Singhai were to arrive.

"Is it so important that I favor one of them?" Fen asked. "Is there more reason to this matchmaking than I am being told?"

"It is your mother's wish," he said.

"I know more men arrived," Fen said. At his mildly surprised look, she explained, "Shen."

"Ah," he nodded, understanding.

"It is not my wish to receive them, but I will do what I am ordered to do," she said.

"Is there another reason your heart is closed to this?" His eyes bore into hers at the question and she found she couldn't look away.

"No," she said.

"Another person?"

"No," she lied, doing her best to put Aaron from her mind. What else could she say? Proclaim her attraction to him to her father, a man who would surely not understand?

"You're sure?"

"*Shi.*" Fen nodded. "I only have no wish for marriage. Mei and Jin have married, isn't that enough to please her? Mei even gave birth to your grandson."

"Don't pretend to misunderstand. You know your mother's heart as well as I. She wishes for you to remain in Muntong, to have babies where she can hold them. Can you really blame her for that?"

"And you?" Fen asked.

"I wish to see you settled with a man worthy of you. If it takes a thousand nobles, I will show them all to you. I would see you happy, with a family, Fen."

Fen cringed inwardly. He was serious. Her father fully intended on parading nobles in front of her until she decided. The prospect of spending years upon years receiving noble guests rolled out in front of her like a bad dream. "And if I don't wish to marry a nobleman?"

"You are a princess, Fen," he said. "You have been raised as a lady. Only a nobleman will know how to cultivate your mind. Trust me when I tell you, any other, those less worthy, will lose their appeal soon after the wedding. The people of Lintian expect more of you. They look to you for a sense of right. We are the gods they can see."

"But Mei—"

"Married a foreign prince, a man whose warrior race make for logical allies in these troubled intergalactic times. What she learns in space may someday save our planet. Besides, she sends back information and downloads for our libraries, in case we ever have to deal with aliens. It's not pleasant business, but it is necessary."

"And Jin?" she asked, knowing her father merely spun the events of Mei's marriage for the sake of the people. That's what the commoners believed.

"Married a historian, a woman with unique knowledge of our people's past," he said. "And it was willed by the gods. We had no choice in the matter. It had to be."

Francesca knew the truth behind the whole Wushu Uprisings, a war that had nearly ended their whole way of life a long time ago. She also practiced the outlawed form of Wushu—a fact few commoners would know.

"What of my brothers?" As soon as she said it, she felt bad. She didn't wish her fate on them. She wanted them to get married in their own time, when they wanted, to whom they wanted.

"Their time will come," he said. "But now is your time."

"Can't the gods will something for me?" Fen asked.

The emperor gave the faintest smile. "And who would they will? I thought you said there was no one to take your interest from the noble suitors."

Caught in her lie, she said, "There isn't. I just would prefer the choice."

"And so you have it—within reason." He still hadn't moved, save for his hand on his long mustache. "I cannot have three of my children so wildly wed. There must be some order to it. The people need a ceremony. They need to see that we are still in control of our emotions and our urges. We are not peasants running around the countryside. Hate it as you might, we have an image to uphold. If that image falls, so does the people's faith in our decisions. I will not give Emperor Song reason to attack."

"Attack?" Fen gasped.

"I was speaking figuratively," he said. "There is no reason for alarm."

Fen wasn't so sure. Was there more of a threat than she was being told?

"Promise me that you will act with your family in mind," he said.

Fen nodded. How could she not?

"Then you will make me very happy." The emperor crossed to her. She stiffened. He lifted his hand, patted her shoulder and then left.

Once she was alone, she whispered, "An? An, are you there?"

It took a moment, but the spirit finally showed herself.

"An, please, you have to tell me. Did you say anything about Aaron to the emperor?" Fen sat up on the bed, reaching as if she could grab the spirit's hands. Her fingers fell through An's body.

"I only told him of the threat. I said nothing of your lover." An looked upset, but Fen didn't have time to deal with her temperamental ancestor right now. No doubt the empress had made her mad again.

Fen sighed in relief. "Please, you have to help me. I need to see Aaron. Do you know where he is?"

"He's in the hall, hanging new silk tapestries. Your mother keeps him busy." An floated down, so it looked as if she sat on the bed.

"I have to see him," Fen said. "I need to see him."

"I would've imagined your father told you not to," An said. When Fen started to ask why she'd think that, she added, "I didn't tell him anything, but by the look on your face, he somehow suspects."

"He didn't specifically say not to see him," Fen said.

"What did he say?"

"He only made me promise to act with my family in mind." Fen knew she was stretching the meaning of her father's words, but she had to see Aaron. She needed to touch him and hold him. In truth, the unknown attacks terrified her. Were they attacks? Or was she just unlucky lately? Aaron made her feel safe, and she had a feeling that her time with him was coming to an end. So help her, she wanted every moment, every kiss, every stolen touch.

"You cannot go to Péng You Hall. It is too early

yet in the day." An closed her eyes, sighing long and loud.

"He cannot come here," Fen said.

"I agree." An opened her eyes. "How about the library? Only your ancestors use it. I can easily clear them from the building."

"How?" Fen asked.

An just grinned and refused to answer.

"What about the keeper?" Fen asked.

"He's not at his post. He sleeps off the effects of drink under one of the Enchanted River bridges."

"All right." Fen nodded, suddenly feeling very happy. "The library. But how...?"

"He'll be compelled," An assured her. "I'll tell the empress she'd better not have him measure for new tapestries in there. She'll send him straightaway just to annoy me. Now start walking."

Fen got off the bed and said, "Thank you, An. I can't tell you how much I appreciate you doing this for me."

"I was alive once, too," An said, by way of an answer. "Now go. Hurry. And don't let anyone see you."

Fen nodded, moving to leave.

"Wait," An said, wrinkling her nose. "On second

thought, you'd better change your gown. That one is stained with blood."

Fen looked at her chest. Her skin was healed, thanks to the medic's laser, but there was indeed still blood on her gown. She nodded, not even caring that she'd had an accident only hours before. The promise of seeing Aaron was powerful enough to cure any fear she might feel.

"The pink one," An ordered, "with the red butterflies. Wear that one."

Fen instantly ran to her wardrobe, placing her hand on the wall to open the hidden compartment that held her gowns. The library was on the other side of the palace grounds, near the front gate. Her hands shook in giddy excitement as she quickly undressed to put on the new gown.

17

Aᴀʀᴏɴ sʟᴏᴡʟʏ ᴡᴀʟᴋᴇᴅ to the palace library. He knew he should be glad that the empress was suddenly finding more work for him to do, when only moments before she'd indicated that they were nearly done with his services. It meant he'd have more time at the palace, more time with Fen.

The palace technically had hundreds of buildings, though some appeared to be joined, and he had to stop and ask for directions once he made it to the front section of the compound. The library was set apart from the rest of the palace, hidden in the corner in a private square. The ground was tiled with concrete blocks, forming a giant dragon out of the stone. Four-tiered terraces, ornately decorated with carved figures and tile work and lined with rows of steps, held the three buildings surrounding the square. The largest was the library itself, situated in the middle.

As Aaron made the climb to the front, he noticed how peaceful this section of the palace was. He saw no servants, no guards or gardeners. The library was empty when he entered. Within the immediate entrance, he saw a portrait of the emperor and empress staring down at him from an imposing height. Then, walking along a hall, he saw more portraits, all royal in appearance. Finally, he came to the end, which opened into the library itself.

He looked for the keeper but didn't see one around. Long rows of thick wood tables sat empty. Rolled scrolls lined the walls in giant columns and in single pillars that reached to the tall, sloped ceiling. Symbols were carved along the shelves, tiny words keeping the texts organized. Many nobles' homes had scroll rooms but nothing quite like this. He wondered at what secrets he might find hidden in the old, dusty parchments.

"*Ni hao*," Aaron said softly, only to say louder, "Hello? Is anyone here? I've come to measure for tapestries by order of the empress."

He didn't receive an answer. Looking around, he wondered where exactly the empress wanted tapestries replaced. He didn't see any, only the columns of old scrolls. Exploring to the far back and not seeing anything, he turned back around to make his way once more through the pillars. Paintings lined what little wall space he did see, and he doubted the empress wanted him to take the paintings down and replace them with silk.

"Maybe I misunderstood," he mumbled to himself. "But I don't understand how. She did say the library."

"Hello?"

He stiffened, his body instantly erupting in pleasure at the sound of Fen's voice. It was like the song of an angel, from the mythology of his father's people, calling to him from above. He stepped out from behind a pillar, bowing. "Princess."

"Aaron."

She smiled rushing forward. His heart soared at the sight. Her gown was tight against her body, corseted with a thick belt. Instantly, she was in his arms, kissing him. When he was away from her, he worried about the way he'd acted, but the second he was with her again, all seemed right.

"I missed you," she said, pulling away from his mouth to sprinkle kisses all over his face.

He pushed her back to look at her. "The empress sent me to measure. Did she...?"

Aaron tried not to get excited, but if her mother sent him, did that mean the empress approved?

"She doesn't know. I arranged for us to be alone. No one knows, don't worry."

Aaron knew he had no room to complain, but it hurt him that they had to hide because of who he was. However, he was no fool as to turn her away, not when he wanted her so badly. The night before had been bliss—not just the sex, but afterward as they talked. So many things seemed to just be between them, not needing to be said. The attraction was there, deep and sure, but there was more, a mental connection, an understanding as natural as their need for air.

Fen's kisses moved to his neck. He tried to resist, had told himself he would so that they may talk more, but as her mouth skimmed his earlobe, he was lost. His body was at instant attention and his hands were roaming along her tight silk corset to pull her closer.

"I think about you all day," Fen admitted. "When the other men are talking, I think of how I long to be with you instead."

Aaron captured her mouth at the confession, kissing her harder. She'd never know the pleasure her words gave him. But part of him wondered if it was better not to feel the pleasure, because such things as this could only lead to pain.

"Do you think about me at all?" she asked.

He smiled. Since a young boy, he wasn't one for talking a lot. The princess seemed to take it as a small offense. Holding her head in his hands, he said, "Always. Forever."

"I'm scared, Aaron."

"Of me?" Aaron asked, surprised.

"Of this," she said. "Of it ending. I feel like I don't get enough time with you. I want to talk to you, learn everything you have to say. I want to know you completely."

He nodded, filled with the same fear. What could he tell her though? They both knew it wouldn't last—not unless she gave up her life as a princess to run away with him. Though his late nights were filled with such fantasies, his reality wasn't. He would never ask her to leave a life of privilege for an existence of uncertainty with him. He could never give her the life she had now.

"Do not think of how little the time, just take pleasure in the time we do have," he said, not wanting to see her sad. He stroked back her hair. It was so soft. Reaching behind her head, he pulled at her hair clasp, causing it to cascade around her shoulders in silken waves. He took a bold step forward. Her body was dwarfed by his and he trapped her against one of the scroll pillars.

Her lovely, dark eyes rose to meet his, burning in their passion for him. His heavy arousal pressed against his tight black pants, aching to be set free. Fen shivered beneath his hands, her breathing deepening. Aaron knew how she liked to be taken—wild and rough. He was her escape from her life as a princess. He didn't treat her like a delicate flower but like how a woman should be treated.

Aaron didn't mind, as his passions matched her own in desperation. He stared deep into her eyes, running his hands down her arms to grab her wrists, instantly pulling them so they were trapped above her head against the hard pillar.

"I want to make love to you in every room of every building of the palace," Fen said.

Aaron smiled at the thought, though he knew there was no way he'd have the chance to make love to her so many times, no matter how he longed to do just that.

Desire pulsed through him. Her nipples were hard against the silk, her breasts held up by the corset belt. As he rocked his hips forward along her soft body, her breath caught only to quicken. He licked his lips, desperately needing to taste her once more.

The smell of her body engulfed him, the scent of flowered perfume. Desperation filled him, desperation in the moment, in the need to have her, to never let go. Part of him wanted to throw her from him, to run and save what little part of himself he had left. It was useless. Fen already possessed so much of him—his body, his soul, even his heart. He never imagined he could love, especially not a princess. When his parents died, he swore never to let anyone in. How did Fen sneak past his guard?

His breath came in heavy pants. Without thought, his lips seared over hers, marking her as his, willing her to feel what he felt. Fen made a small noise of approval at his rough embrace and kissed him back with just as much passion. Their tongues clashed and fought in a silent battle between them.

He pressed her body tight against the pillar, holding her wrists captive in one palm. With his free hand, he tugged at her gown, lifting the pink and red silk to expose her legs. When he couldn't free their bodies fast enough, he let go of her wrists and pulled at his waistband. The breeches fell to his ankles, pooling at his feet. Fen held her hands above her head, waiting for him to come back to her. Aaron lifted her skirt, baring her glistening sex. She didn't wear any underclothes.

Aaron moaned softly. He brought his body to hers, again grabbing her wrists as he drew the tip of his shaft to her. With his free hand, he lifted her leg, nestling his shaft close to her moist slit. He thrust himself along her wet folds, feeling the glide of her cream on him.

Closing his eyes, he pushed up, filling her tight and ready body. Fen was always so wet for him. He thrust several times, keeping her arms pinned before he was forced to let her go. Taking her hips, he lifted her up, angling her body so he could go deeper. She pulled at her bodice, disheveling it as she exposed a sweet breast for his lips. Aaron instantly kissed it, sucking the hard nipple as he pumped into her willing folds.

"Ah," Fen cried, as if she didn't care if anyone heard her. She dug her hands into his shoulders, using him for support as he plunged in and out, in an out, fast and hard. Her body slid along the wall. She stiffened, whimpering beautifully as her muscles clenched his cock like a vise. As she shook with release, he couldn't hold back. His body exploded into her, coming so hard his stomach clenched and a loud groan was wrenched from his throat. He stared at her for a long moment, breathing hard as he took in her flushed cheeks and her sated expression.

"I love you," he whispered, unable to keep the words back. He had told himself he'd never confess it, never burden her with his heart. "I love you, Fen."

For a long, stunned moment she stared at him. His body was still deep inside her and her arms were around his neck. "Blessed ancestors help me, but I love you, too, Aaron. I love you, too."

Fen leaned forward, capturing his mouth with hers. His body was spent, but he poured everything he had into that bittersweet kiss. What they had could never be, no matter how he dared to hope that it could. The empress made it clear that he wasn't good enough for the princess.

Aaron rocked his hips, working gently inside her. Only too late did he remember having released inside her. With poorer women, it wasn't a good idea, but surely Fen would be on some sort of birth control. The rich normally were.

Fen moaned, deepening the kiss as the arousal rekindled itself between them.

"Ahhh!"

The high-pitched screech resounded over the library. Dazed with passion, he pulled back to look at

Fen. Her eyes were wide, yet hazy. In unison, they turned toward the empty tables.

The empress stood, her face white as she stared at them.

Fen pushed at his arm, moaning in horror as he let her down. As Fen righted her clothes, Aaron pulled his pants to his waist to hide his wilting member.

"Fen," the empress said, her voice hard and abnormally loud. Her mouth worked, as if too horrified by what she'd seen to let any words pass through.

"It's not..." Fen began, breathless.

Aaron looked at her, part of him hurt by her automatic denial of the obvious. Her eyes met his and she shook her head. Was she saying she was sorry?

18

FEN STOOD before her mother in mortification. It was bad enough she'd been caught having sex in the library, but worse that it was with a man who wasn't a suitor or a nobleman. Even after her chest was covered, she still grabbed the silk as if doing so would hide her sudden shame.

"You disgrace your family," the empress said. "How could you do this, Fen? With willing, appropriate suitors lining up to marry you? What if they walked in here and saw you with him? Have you thought of your reputation? Of the family's? What are you thinking?"

"It's not unheard of to take lovers," she said weakly.

"It is unheard of when the emperor orders you not to," her mother answered.

"He didn't order me to stay away from Aaron." Fen knew she shouldn't be arguing with her mother, but she couldn't help herself. Inside, her heart felt like it was being squeezed of all life. She hadn't lied when she'd said she loved him.

The empress scowled and turned her eyes to Aaron, "I specifically ordered you to stay away from the royal princess. I could have you imprisoned for the rest of your life for disobeying me."

"No." Fen stepped forward, hiding Aaron behind her back.

"Princess, please, do not take my shame unto yourself," Aaron said quietly.

"It is a little late for that," the empress said. "Your own grandmother has disowned you. Did he tell you that, Fen? Not only is his station unworthy of you, his honor is as well. He has no family, no true name."

"I have a name," Aaron said, his voice hardening. Fen was proud of him for speaking up, yet fearful at the same time. Doing so would only convince the empress to have him truly imprisoned or worse, exiled. "I have my father's name. Piers."

"Foreign space trash," the Empress declared. "A *yang gui zi* whose family is all dead, killed by common raiders like common space port trash. Of course we know of it, Aaron. We make it our business to know who is coming to the palace. Lady Hsin was kind enough to fill us in on your past. You are lucky a woman as great as Lady Hsin took pity on you, but such luck does not last if it is not earned."

"My father was a good man," Aaron protested.

"And you are not," the empress yelled.

Fen looked at Aaron, wondering why he didn't deny that his family had disowned him. Such a thing was rare, and his sin must have been great indeed. Why hadn't he told her?

Then, as she thought of it, she realized they hadn't done as much talking as maybe they should have. In her heart, she'd felt that they knew each other without all the words. Her heart had been wrong. Her love was a romantic girlhood notion, a desperate cry to escape her fate, her duty, her marriage to a nobleman. Knowing it was such didn't kill the pain.

And Aaron. His motive for loving her was suddenly clear. He had nothing but a past bad enough to get him kicked out of his own family. Why *wouldn't* he say he loved her? She represented everything he didn't have—money, power, honor. To a man like him, logic would say that she had the power to give him everything he'd lost. He could vindicate himself as her lover. For, if a royal princess of the Zhang Dynasty thought enough of him to take him to her bed, then surely he was worthy.

The awful truth hit her. He was using her for his own gain. As a young girl, her life teachers had warned her about such men, warned her that she would be under special attack because of her position.

She thought herself smart, but in that moment, she felt like a stupid little girl.

Fen looked at him, her eyes watering with the agony of his betrayal, even as a part of her heart screamed that he could do no such thing, that he could never betray her no matter what logic said. His handsome face was blank as he met her stare. She waited for him to speak, to deny what her mother was saying, but he didn't.

Finally, he turned his eyes to the floor and did not look up again.

"Fen," the empress ordered. "Come."

Fen didn't move as she stared at him.

"I said come." The empress' voice rose with her anger.

Fen finally joined her mother, her feet shuffling in dejection.

"Piers Aaron, you will go immediately to your chambers and stay there. If you do not, I'll order the guards to kill you on sight."

He placed fist to palm and bowed dutifully. The empress didn't even watch his agreement as she roughly jerked Fen's arm, dragging her daughter toward the library entrance. Fen stumbled to keep up with the hurried pace.

Once they reached the outside steps, the empress slowed to a more regal walk, her head held high as if she hadn't a care in the world. All sign of emotion was gone from her features, replaced by the calm, cool look Fen associated with her mother.

"Empress," Fen said, keeping her tone quiet. Even now, she was worried about Aaron. Threatening to kill him wasn't an idle thing with her mother. If she decreed it, she'd do it. "Mother, please. What will you do?"

"That will be up to the emperor," the empress answered.

"You will tell him everything?" Fen gasped, horrified that her father would know about what she'd done.

"You are a disobedient, willful daughter, Fen," her mother said. "We've offered you every chance and when we expect some decorum in return, you dishonor yourself and your family."

"I meant, what will you do to him?" she asked.

"I ordered him to stay away from you. I told him that you were busy with suitors and still he disobeyed me, his empress. What do you think I should do? What would the law have me do?" The empress stopped at the bottom of the steps. Their words were hushed but Fen could easily hear the anger in her mother's tone. "Lady Hsin will have to be warned against such an employee. I will not tell her the details of it and shame our family more, but she was kind to give him a second chance and must be told the truth of who she hired."

Fen wrung her hands before her waist, tugging at her wrinkled gown to make it more presentable for the walk across the palace grounds. Never had it seemed so long a distance as it did now.

"She, naturally, will exile him from her lands, but it will not be necessary."

"What do you mean?" Fen asked. "You will kill him?"

"I am not so barbaric as that," the empress said. "Besides, to do so would make his shame and yours known. The family does not need such scandal, not now with so many nobles within our walls."

"Then...?" Fen couldn't bring herself to hate him, even though she was angry about his not telling her the full truth of who he was—a dishonored man. But more than the anger, she was terrified—scared she'd never see him again, that he'd be hurt, that her heart would never recover. She wanted to hate him, but it wasn't in her. Confusion set in, coursing through her mind.

"I knew when the treacherous An tried to taunt me into getting new tapestries for the library that she was up to something. She thinks me a fool, but I know well the décor of my own palace, even if I do not frequent all the buildings in it."

They came to the end of the tiled private square. Fen glanced up at the two fierce creatures that guarded the entryway. Their angry yawns were frozen in white stone, as each held out a large claw-filled paw.

"An better be careful, lest she finds her soul exorcised from these walls."

"Mother, no, you mustn't! An is not at fault. I am," Fen said. She'd never seen her mother this angry. "I'm a grown woman. I make my own decisions."

"That *yang gui zi* has caused enough trouble," the empress said. "You are not to see him again. Ever.

And that is a royal order from your empress, make no mistake."

"*Shi*," Fen said, reluctantly agreeing.

"If you were not my daughter, Fen..." The empress let the threat taper off. "You allowed Lord He to leave here insulted and our relations with the Song Dynasty are even more troubled than they already were. Your brother Haun has been working hard to keep peace, as has the emperor. Already we must send Haun back to the Song palace to keep the peace between our two lands. There is so much at stake that you don't know, Fen."

"I know, Mother," Fen said. She shivered, remembering her father hinting at an attack. Was there much that was being kept from her? What didn't she know? How could she be so in the dark? Was there another reason, a reason that had to do with her welfare should the Zhang Dynasty come under attack, that made her mother so desperate to see her settled?

"You do not know, daughter," the empress said, confirming her suspicions.

"Then tell me, please. What is happening? What is being kept from me?" Fen tried to stop walking, going as far as to touch her mother's arm.

The empress pulled away, continuing down the

path. "You have been told all that you need to be told. I see no point in taking you into my confidence now. You can't obey the little requests we've already laid at your feet."

Little? Her mother considered the command that she pick a man for marriage *little*?

"Lord He feels his honor has been insulted and after Piers Aaron's actions, I tend to believe Lord He has a right to be."

"Empress?" Fen didn't like the diminishing anger in her mother's voice, the slight fall of tone she got when coming to a conclusion.

"Aaron will be exiled to Singhai, delivered to Lord He to be dealt with as the noble sees fit."

"He'll kill him," Fen gasped.

"I doubt it. He'll most likely make him a servant. Really, it is the most humane course. Aaron will have a new profession. Once Lady Hsin fires him, he'll not find work in Muntong."

Fen stopped walking, not caring that her mother kept going down the path. Aaron fated to be a servant in Lord He's home? She'd heard rumors of how such servants were treated in Singhai. Lord He would have Aaron beaten, starved, tortured, imprisoned, castrated...

Tianna!

"No," Fen said, loud enough that her mother heard her.

The empress stopped, turning in surprise, her mouth open as if she'd still been talking, completely unaware that her daughter wasn't next to her.

Fen rushed forward, shaking her head in denial. "No, you can't do that."

"I most certainly can and will," the empress assured her.

"Then I won't get married," Fen said. "*Ever*. I'll die just as I am now, unwed and living in the Royal Hall. You will get no grandchildren out of me."

"And if I don't?" the empress asked.

"I'll..." Fen paused. "I'll choose a husband out of the nobles you brought here to the palace. We'll give my choice to the astrologers so they can consult their *Chien Tung* or whatever divination tool they need to use to declare the match fitting. I'm sure you can convince them to give their blessing to whomever I pick."

"I would never presume to know more than fate," the empress denied, insulted.

"Fine, but even fate can be read differently according to circumstance," Fen said. "Give me your word that you will say nothing about Aaron to Lady Hsin or to the emperor. Send him home, his honor as intact as it was before he came. No one knows of what I've done. If you do this, I will choose a husband."

The empress studied her face for a long moment before slowly smiling. "Ye Shing—"

"I will choose the husband," Fen said, sternly. "My decision. But I promise it will be one of the nobles."

The empress nodded. "Choose well. We'll make the announcement tonight as we dine."

"Tonight?" Fen was nauseated at just the thought.

"*Shi.*" The empress nodded. "Tonight."

What did it matter if she chose tonight or next week? In the end, it was all the same. She'd be married. Any number of her suitors would make a fine husband and a deep friendship would come in time.

"I'll be in my chambers, preparing myself." Fen bowed to her mother. She saw movement in the corner of her eye and glanced back to see Aaron. The distance kept his exact expression from her, but he stopped walking.

"You are not to see him," the empress said, her voice gentle. "Trust me, Fen, it's for the best. Such affairs as these have no future, only a shameful past.

Nothing good can come from anything that man has offered you."

Fen glanced at her mother and nodded her head, saying nothing. Sure, the woman could be understanding now that she'd finally gotten her way.

Fen was the first to walk away, not daring to look at Aaron, unable to see him now that her future was set. There would be no goodbyes for them, no final kiss or touch. All that happened would be but a memory, a song carried on the wind only to be heard on lonely nights when one couldn't help but remember what could have been.

A tear slipped over her cheek and she quickened her pace. Her pain needed the solitude of her bedchamber, away from the palace eyes. First, she would cry. Then she would lock away her heart and choose her future with logic and wisdom, and then she'd take the next step in her lifelong journey with the poise of a true Zhang princess.

19

Why? Why!

After all his patience, why wasn't Princess Fen his? He'd borne her infidelity with a servant, he'd sacrificed his own blood to his ancestors for help. And now this, the final insult. She was to marry another.

"Please, blessed ancestors, help the rumors to be lies. Or, if not lies, help her to pick me, her true husband. How can she do this to me? Treating me as if I were no more than a wood post she can lean on and forget." The man rocked back and forth, tears streaming from his eyes—hot trails of frustration. "Make it not so. Make it not so."

He rocked faster, pulling at his hair in frustration. The walls of his chamber in Péng You Hall started to loom in on him, wobbling under his vision as if they were about to collapse. The walls stayed standing, but the sick feeling of hopelessness within him didn't go away.

"I am not wood. I am not wood. Help her to see. Help her to know the truth. I have survived all tests, borne all grief. Please, show her the truth. Let her see me, her wooden post, let her see. *Make* her see."

"Fen, it's not true, is it?" Shen asked, coming around the corner into the imperial gardens where she sat alone. Lian and Haun were right behind him. "Rumors are flying all over the palace. The empress said you had chosen a husband and that it would be announced tonight."

"No," Fen said in dejection.

"Then she misunderstood something," Haun said. "Quick, come with us so that we may find her and stop her madness."

"No," Fen said. "I will announce a husband tonight. I just haven't decided on who that man will be."

"Why?" Lian asked. They stopped near her bench, towering over her, their stances wide as they stood, arms crossed over their chests. They made a pretty intimidating sight. She wasn't scared.

Fen looked at the ground, bombarded with their protective presence but not feeling like she could move. After an hour crying in her chambers, she'd been forced to leave as servants came to clean. They assumed her red puffy eyes were from tears of joy, as a bride's tears were a lucky sign.

"What happened?" Haun asked.

"How is she forcing your hand?" Shen demanded. He closed his eyes, as if trying to see the future. "I know she's up to something. You wouldn't have changed your mind so fast. You are more constant than that."

"No, Shen, stop trying to read into it," Fen said "Don't look at it. I don't want to know anything about what will happen."

Shen opened his eyes and nodded. He sat down beside her. "Who will you choose, Fen? And why?"

"Mou Tian," Fen said, knowing that out of all of them, he'd be the least interested in an intimate relationship with her. She couldn't imagine taking another man to her bed. Ever.

"No," Haun said, his tone closely resembling an order. "Why would you take such a man? There is no logic in the decision."

"I think him perfect. I do not want a marriage and he does not want me." Fen shrugged delicately and looked up.

"You are upset," Lian said. "You wouldn't be saying this if you were thinking clearly."

"If you are set on this course, at least give yourself a chance at a happy life. Pick a man you can come to love, Fen," Haun said. "It's not like your options are limited."

"But they are." She laughed wryly. Out of all of them, it didn't surprise her that Haun would be the first to accept her decision. He knew about duty, about sacrificing himself for his people. As future emperor, he would marry someone who was best for the empire, not someone who was best for his heart. It was the way of things for him. Haun never complained, never spoke of it, but Fen felt sorry for him. They all did.

"She caught you with someone? That's how she's forcing you to do this," Lian said. She should've known he'd figure it out with his gift of the present. "Your heart feels like it's been crushed into small pieces." He took a deep breath, touching her arm and gasping. "It's broken, Fen. What's happened?"

"Don't read me," Fen demanded, standing. "I told you I don't want to know anything."

"Fen, okay, we understand. If you say you must do this, then we'll support your decision. But, not Mou Tian, all right? Pick another. Pick anyone, so long as you give yourself a chance to be happy." Shen stood with her.

Lian pressed his hand over his heart. He was breathing hard as he stared at her. She couldn't meet his eyes.

"Pick someone you could see loving," Lian said. "If not now, in the times to come."

"Give yourself a chance at happiness," Haun added. "We all know you would never do this if you didn't feel you had to."

"Duty and honor," Fen whispered, looking at Haun. His expression clouded. She now truly knew how he felt. How did he deal with it? "It's all we are in this life, isn't it? We're royalty. We're gods the people can see. And because they expect it, we must be who they want us to be. Duty and honor."

Her brothers didn't answer. Haun nodded once, a slow, deliberate motion that stated he both agreed and understood.

"Who would you have me choose?" she asked. "You three love me more than anyone else in this palace. You will want my happiness even when I don't care to look for it. Who would you choose for me if the choice were yours? Ye Shing?"

"Deng Li," Shen said. "His future is untroubled and bright."

"Deng Li," Lian added. "He likes you and he is a kind, good man. He knows respect and will make a fine father to your children."

Fen turned to Haun. The phoenix blessed the oldest with strength and a warrior's heart. He was brave, sturdy and did what had to be done. He, out of all her family, would understand her position and sacrifice. He would know what she had to do. "And you, Haun? Who would you pick for me?"

"I agree," Haun said. "Deng Li will make a fine husband. He will take care of you, Fen. Chang-shangu is a fine province. If you choose to live there and not at the palace, I can see you making a happy life for yourself. As far as fates go, it's not so bad a one."

"Then I bow to your gifts, brothers, and thank you for your council." Fen took a deep breath and looked at them each in turn. "For this is not a deci-sion I can make for myself right now."

20

Aaron opened the chamber door, surprised to see a palace servant standing before him and not a guard. His stomach was in knots—not so much because of his fate, but for Fen's. He didn't care what happened to him, so long as she wasn't punished. Luckily, as a princess, she would most likely be forgiven, her *shame* hidden within a secret. Aaron was used to being a secret.

He'd seen Fen's face when the empress told her of his past, of how he'd been disowned. What the empress hadn't said, is that he'd been a boy when it happened, newly delivered onto an unhappy grandmother's doorstep.

"The emperor and empress request your presence during dinner," the servant said, interrupting his thoughts.

Aaron nodded, not saying anything as he shut the door. There was no request to the command. He didn't have a choice. He was going to dinner. Confused, he shook his head. Dinner? Why dinner?

It was too much to hope that the empress had changed her mind about him. He'd seen the judgment in her eyes. It was a look he was familiar with, a look that said he was unworthy.

Lying down on the bed, he tried to breathe over the rock his heart had become. It was truly over with Fen, and the pain was much worse than he thought it would be.

FEN SMILED AT DENG LI, but it was a halfhearted attempt. He really was a nice man, with a kind manner, dark steady eyes and a handsome face. His dark hair was cut short, barely a half of an inch long on top. When he spoke, his voice was melodious, the kind of voice a woman could easily listen to without getting tired of. She was making a good choice. He would make a compassionate, smart and talented husband. What woman could really ask for more?

Love.

"I wish to speak to you," Fen said, motioning to a bench randomly placed along the long walkway near a row of shrubs. She ignored the thoughts in the back of her mind, telling her she deserved love, happiness...Aaron.

"Are you sure?" Li asked, his sober expression saying he understood what she was going to ask him.

She sighed in relief, grateful that he wasn't going to make her explain in detail. "Yes. I feel we could be happy."

"Then it is my duty to accept," he said with a firm nod.

Fen sat, motioning him to join her. He did, taking his place at her side but leaving enough room so their bodies did not touch. She eyed him carefully, almost pitying him. He was so nice, so deserving, and she resented herself for not loving him.

There is something to be said about friendship in marriage. Love will come in time.

Fen closed her eyes and took a deep breath, doing her best to hide the pain inside her chest. "Do not accept only out of duty. I will not pretend to feel something I don't, and you must make your decision freely. This is not a royal decree. If you refuse, no one will know, not even the emperor."

Li looked at his hands, considering her words.

"Speak openly, please," she said.

"I would know why you do this."

"I'm not being given a choice," Fen answered. She figured that was enough of an explanation. How could she speak of emotions she had yet to consider fully, had yet to get over? Even now, looking at Li, she didn't feel attraction. She didn't feel the burning need, the desperate pull she did with Aaron. "But you are. I don't want you to accept if you feel your happiness can be discovered elsewhere. I choose you because you are kind. You will make a good leader to the people, a good husband. And, if anyone is to benefit from marriage to a princess, I wish it to be a man who deserves whatever benefits such an alliance will bring."

"I am flattered by your words," he said, finally meeting her eyes. "I am here out of duty, and I've stayed for the same reason. Each suitor knows why he is here, Princess. A man could hardly wish for more admirable qualities in a wife. I would be honored."

Fen nodded. He hesitated, reaching forward to touch her hand. It was awkward, but she let him hold it. "My mother wishes to make an announcement tonight. The astrologers will be consulted, but I can't remember them ever saying no to a match. They give warnings such as no babies the first year and whatnot, but never have they said no. Not even with my brother, Jin, did they disclaim the match."

Li nodded, patting her hand. They sat back and she was relieved that being with him was at least comfortable. He didn't make her talk and she was glad. She didn't think she could hold a conversation right now anyway.

21

MADAME ENG, the head of the four other palace astrologers, was already in the dining hall when Fen arrived. A long table had been set up, showcasing the many ways they were to divine her future. As Fen tried not to look at the table, she wished her sister Mei was home. Having brothers was fine, but she really needed a woman to talk to—one who wasn't her mother.

There were no guards in the hall, only the noble guests. Not only was the first batch of suitors there, so was the second—men she'd met over the years during royal ceremonies. Just like the first group, they ranged in age and qualities. She felt nothing for them as she was reintroduced.

Dinner was a long affair and Fen did not have the

appetite for it. She spent most of her time pushing her food around her plate with her *kuay tzu*. The carved ivory chopsticks were only used on special occasions.

Li sat next to her, nodding occasionally in encouragement. He sensed how hard this was for her, and she imagined it wasn't the easiest for him. Everyone dreamed of a marriage filled with passion and love. Her intended looked handsome in the ceremonial green chinoiserie jacket with frog fastenings and a Mandarin collar. The buttons were undone, and beneath the jacket was a cream and white buttoned shirt.

It didn't take much to conclude that her mother was responsible for the outfit, for the green matched the lighter green of her gown, though hers was embroidered with blue flowers slashing across the chest. Again, the empress picked a style that forced the air from Fen's lungs. The belt was cinched tight, keeping her back rigid and her ribs sore.

She probably doesn't want to give me the chance to make a run for it, Fen thought.

Her hair was left long and loose about her shoulders. In truth, she didn't have the willpower to do anything with it, so she'd just left it after stepping out of the decontaminator.

Lord Ye sat brooding, his eyes refusing to lift from the table as he drank. Fen couldn't find the strength to care that he was miserable in her choice. It wasn't like she relished making it. Shing seemed to take it all in stride. Yuan was as indifferent as ever, talking to his brother and no one else, beyond saying a few sentences in answer to some question.

It took her a moment, but she realized one of the suitors was missing. Fei Bin. He normally was punctual, not that she could remember much else about him.

Chu Dun and Tan Ho looked disappointed, but not overly upset as they made jokes and tried to liven the mood of the somber table. Unfortunately, with his soft voice, Ho couldn't be heard over the entire table.

Chi Tan's expression matched Lord Ye's, as if they couldn't understand why they hadn't been picked above all others. This irritated her, because they almost acted as if this was some game to be won and not a marriage to be had. It made her wonder what would've happened after the wedding if she'd have chosen them. Would the fun be over and would they be off to the next sport?

Fen took a deep breath, trying not to be overly

harsh in judging the men. It wasn't their fault none of them was Aaron.

Aaron.

He never felt so far away as he did now. She was engaged to another. His honor was blemished by some deed of his past. Fen wanted to ask her mother for details, but the woman would hardly welcome the queries. The empress would not lie about such a thing, and Aaron didn't make one sound to defend himself, which could only mean it was true. It must have been a seedy thing indeed to make a grandmother turn out her grandson.

Fen had even tried asking An, but the spirit knew nothing about it. Though, she was angry with Fen for conceding to the empress' wishes.

Her heart automatically wanted to romanticize the situation, giving her head excuses, telling her that he could've changed from the man he was. The facts were there, but she didn't know them all. Regardless, she couldn't let her heart rule her head. It didn't matter anyway. She was to be married and Aaron would be kept safe, far away from Lord He's reaching talons.

After the *shui guo cha* was served and they all sat around the long table sipping the spiced tea, the empress drew their attention to the astrologers.

Madame Eng's green silk gown had long sleeves that trailed to the floor. The outfit matched those of the other astrologers—all short, tiny old women who shuffled their feet when they walked. The only contrast was Madame Bing, whose rounded frame stuck out when they filed along in a straight line.

Suddenly, her eyes were drawn to movement in the corner. Without really seeing him, she sensed him. It was Aaron.

What was he doing here? The full impact of her choice hit her like a kick to the chest. She turned her rounded eyes to her mother, doing her best to keep the tremor from her hand and the pain from her face.

The empress was already approaching her. Fen stood without waiting to be beckoned. At once, Li was by her side, coughing slightly.

Her mother must have read her confused expression, for she nodded once. Pulling her arm, the empress drew Fen aside and whispered, "A royal pardon for a royal announcement."

Fen wondered if her mother had planned this as part of her punishment. Or perhaps this was her way of ensuring all ties between them were severed. No man who witnessed a woman's betrothal would dare make advances toward her without fear of repercussions from her intended.

"Madame Eng," Fen said. The hall was quiet and her quivering voice resounded over it. "It is my wish..." She paused as she felt Li take her elbow, touching her gently. Glancing at him, she amended, "It is our wish to marry. Please tell us if it is to be a blessed and happy match."

This was all for the sake of ceremony, but the empress clearly wanted it all down. Fen noticed a scholar recording her words. Until she stood, she hadn't seen him behind the table.

"It would be an honor, Princess," Madame Eng said. "Many blessings."

"Many blessings." The rejected suitors toasted halfheartedly, lifting their glasses.

"A true honor." Madame Bing shyly started to step forward but drew back behind the others at the last second.

"A great honor." Madame Kel waved her hand to the side before placing it over her heart.

"We will use all our powers to ensure your happiness," Madame Chaim added, grinning widely.

"A true and great honor," Madame Cong agreed, nodding smartly. She was a bit of a busybody who liked to be before crowds, as was evident by the slightly overpowering thunder of her tone. "And one we take with great seriousness."

"Thank you," Fen said. The palace scholar recorded every word, writing on his electronic clipboard at a fevered pace.

"We look to your wisdom and your guidance," the empress said. Fen glanced at her, mildly annoyed by the interruption. Apparently, her mother didn't think she was putting on a good enough show for the other suitors.

The women busied themselves, looking over notes and scrolls. Fen tried not to look toward Aaron's shadowed corner, but it didn't change her awareness of his presence.

Fen knew they'd already prepared their answer and wasn't surprised when, after some time and fiddling, Madame Eng announced, "We have consulted the charts. The couple is well matched in age, birthdates, and birth hours."

"There might be some tension in the home with the two signs," Madame Bing added in caution, "but only if the marriage is not tended like a garden."

Madame Kel was next, her eyes narrowing. "Odds would be best if they married soon."

"Very soon," Madame Chaim added.

"Wait," Madame Bing said, pointing to a chart. "This conflicts that point."

"What?" Madame Eng asked. All the women

crowded around the chart. Madame Eng reached out and brushed her hand across it, wiping it clean. "Ah, that makes more sense."

"We asked the ancestors for guidance," Madame Cong said. "They were unclear."

"What of the bones?" the empress inserted quickly, no doubt not wanting Zhang An to have any say in the matter.

"Ah, favorable," Madame Chaim said.

"So said the shells from the Satlyun." Madame Kel nodded wisely.

"And your conclusion?" the empress asked.

"There is one more thing to consult. The *Chien Tung*." Madame Eng stepped around the table, reaching into her gown for the bamboo sticks.

Eng suddenly tripped, stumbling forward. The wooden sticks flew out at the couple, hitting both Fen and Li before falling to the floor.

The astrologers gasped, rushing forward to help Eng off the floor. Once to her feet, Madame Eng brushed off their hands. She turned to the princess, an apology started—only to freeze, staring at Fen's head.

Fen reached up, feeling a stick in her hair. She pulled it out and looked at its markings. They didn't mean anything to her. She reached forward to hand it to Eng.

The astrologer shook, hesitating before taking it and turning to the others.

They whispered in a frenzy of gestures and moans before addressing the hall once more. "We are sorry, but this match cannot be. If you were to marry, it would result in a quick death."

Fen was too stunned to move. Never in all her years had she heard of the astrologers turning down a match. Sometimes they warned against certain elements, giving advice, but never had they said a flat no.

"What?" the empress gasped. She turned to the table and waved her hands. Fen watched the men file out of the dining hall. Lord Ye openly smiled at her, but she was too stunned to notice if his excitement was shared by all.

Fen looked toward the corner for Aaron. He was still there. Relief flooded her at the realization, yet she worried that harm might befall him at this unexpected change.

"You said the signs were favorable," the empress said. The emperor stood beside her, quietly listening. Aside from her parents, the astrologers and her questionable fiancé, Fen and Aaron were the only others left in the room—unless he stood with someone she couldn't see. She wondered why Aaron stayed. He pressed against the wall, holding still as if not to be noticed.

"This," Madame Eng held up the stick that she'd gotten from Fen's hair, "is death. Never in my days have I pulled this stick, and now it lands on your daughter as she stands next to Deng Li."

"Combined with what we know, it is clear that if Princess Fen marries Deng Li, she will die within two moons," Madame Chaim announced with certainty, staring down at the fallen sticks as they lay scattered on the floor. "It is very clear."

"Very." Madame Cong pursed her lips tightly together as she too studied the fallen sticks.

Fen turned to look at Li. He smiled at her and took her hand. Very quietly, he said, "I am sorry, Princess. Your life is not a risk I could take. Thank you for gracing me with your proposal and let us part as friends."

Fen nodded. "Of course."

Li bowed to her before doing the same to the astrologers and then the royal couple. He took his leave, saying, "I will leave you to this family affair."

When he was gone, Madame Eng added, "There is more."

"More that has nothing to do with marriage," Madame Cong said.

"The princess' life is in danger," Madame Kel said.

"Grave danger." Madame Bing stepped forward, only to pull back behind the others.

"She must be taken from the palace, for there is one here who would see her harmed," Madame Chaim said.

"A cold, cold spirit." Madame Eng shivered visibly.

"Controlled by one who is close to the princess," Madame Kel added.

"Someone close to me wishes to do me harm?" Fen asked, shocked. They'd suspected someone was after her, but someone close?

She looked at Aaron in the corner, wanting to run to him.

"I see," the empress said. Fen's gaze gave Aaron away. Her mother stiffened, staring at the man a little longer than necessary.

"Empress?" Fen shook her head in denial when her mother glanced at her. Aaron was not trying to kill her. No part of her could believe that.

"Princess Fen must be protected," Madame Chaim said.

"Please, ladies," the empress said, "go consult all your powers. We must know more."

The astrologers readily agreed, leaving the hall in a flurry of hushed tones.

"I think it would be best if I visit Jin," Fen said.

"And leave the palace?" the empress demanded. "But we can protect you. We have guards."

"And Francesca can defeat every one of our guards," Fen reminded her. "I'll be safe with her. Please." Fen turned her eyes to her father, who'd been abnormally quiet. "Please, Emperor. I do not feel safe here. Let me go to Jin and Francesca in disguise. There, I can hide out."

"*Shi*, I think that might be best," the emperor said.

"And if that doesn't work out, I'll see if Mei won't take me with her into—"

"No." The empress cut her off immediately. "You are not going into space with your sister. You are staying on Lintian. Nothing good comes from going into space."

Don't worry, Empress. If I went to space, I'd be running away from marriage, not into it.

"What will we say?" the empress asked.

"That Fen is purifying herself," the emperor said.

"No, then it will be assumed that she had sins to

atone for." Her mother's cutting glance pierced her with its intensity. "We will say she is ill."

"Fine," the emperor said. "But a short illness. We don't want people to think she's sickly."

The emperor gave her a small smile before quickly hiding it from his wife.

"*Shi*, then she will have reason to purify herself if she was ill." The empress nodded in agreement. "Haun should escort her. When the astrologers determine that the threat is out of the palace, we will bring her back and she will wed..." Her mother gave her an expectant look.

"Um, Ye Shing," Fen said, using the first name that popped into her head.

The empress smiled in pleasure.

"But, we should wait to tell anyone," Fen said, causing her mother's happy expression to fade. "I don't want to appear desperate for a husband. Think of our reputation."

For once, the excuse of family honor was going to work in her favor.

"*Shi*, you are right." Still, the empress didn't seem too happy about it.

"I will send for Haun," the emperor said, walking away.

"I don't see why you're upset," Fen told her

mother when they were alone. "We had a bargain and I will stick to it. You send Aaron home and I will marry one of your noblemen. What difference is it to you whether it is tomorrow or in ten moons?"

"Ten?" The empress shook her head. "Don't think you're putting it off that long, daughter. I guarantee we'll have everyone in the palace searched and the culprit discovered long before then."

"Ten moons was just a random number, Mother," Fen said, shaking her head. "Besides, I tried to marry Deng Li. You can't blame me if fate had other plans."

IF THE EMPRESS had wanted to torture him, she'd picked the perfect thing. Watching Fen announce that she wanted to marry another man was agony. He couldn't hear what was happening now, only saw the look on Fen's face. Her skin was pale, her eyes round, and she didn't look happy. Had she wanted to marry the man who now walked away, who left her alone?

"Blessed ancestors help me, but I love you, too, Aaron. I love you, too."

Her words echoed inside him, playing over and over in his head. Had they been a lie? His heart didn't want to believe it, but really, what did he know about the princess? What besides the image the public saw and the woman who came to him in seduction? They hadn't talked, not really. No promises had been made.

But her beautiful dark eyes, they were so clear, so kind. And when she'd said she loved him, she had meant it. He had to believe that, for when she said the words, his whole world seemed to have meaning, and he felt something that he hadn't felt since being a small child—pure happiness.

Love or not, they were not meant to be. She was a princess and he was a disowned peasant. Even if it wasn't so, he'd never be worthy of her. How could a mortal man ever be worthy of a perfect butterfly?

22

Fen smiled for the first time since being caught in the library with Aaron two days before. The wind blew her hair back from her head as the large craft hovered over the meadows, sailing past the lush Lintianese countryside to take her away from Honorable City. She'd wanted to leave immediately after the prediction, but security measures had to be taken. Haun had taken care of everything. He had checked the land craft to make sure it wasn't compromised, planned the route they would take, and decided which servants could be trusted to help with their departure.

The *tu di hang,* land craft, was designed after the ancient junk ships of Old Earth. The large sails harnessed the wind, giving speed with the help of the solar panels hidden in the dark wood. The panels were so small they couldn't be seen by human eyes.

The dark brown wood was accented with gold and red, and an eye was painted on one side next to the Lintianese character for the Zhang family name. The eye actually hid a sensor that read their palms so that it could never be stolen—or in the case of a very young Haun, never again be taken out for a joyride. It was his little midnight trips that had inspired the lock on the royal family's *tu di hang*.

Fen leaned against the rail, letting her silk gown flutter in the breeze as she stood on the oval deck, high on a platform that overlooked the distance. She'd worn a cloak to disguise her as they left the palace—just in case any saw them go in the early morning hours.

The wooden belly of the craft brushed the taller blades of yellow-blue grass, making a swooshing noise as they sped past. The red of the giant *hong jio ju* flowers blended against the blades, leading the eye to a forest nestled in the distant horizon. Three stiff canvas sails were unfurled overhead. Their large span cast shadows over the deck. A heavy anchor hung from the front, used mostly in case of a windstorm when the craft needed to be secured. They never got windstorms in the palace, but out on the open plains the harsher weather was more common.

Haun stood at the helm, just down a small row of steps from her, quietly watching the land drift by. The craft had self-navigation, but Haun often turned it off in favor of driving it himself. Fen figured it was because he was used to always being in control. They were far from the palace, but close to the place Jin and Francesca were to call home.

A cluster of farmhouses formed a village. They sailed past and Fen marveled at the beauty of their dark walls against the pale blue sky. It was these moments of freedom from the palace that made her remember just how much of a paradise Lintian could be.

"It makes you wonder why the palace has walls, doesn't it?" Haun asked from her side. His hair whipped violently about his head and the dark silk of his long tunic shirt pressed tight against his chest.

Fen jolted in mild surprise to hear his voice but smiled in answer. "I know the walls are to keep people out, but often I feel as if they're trapping me in."

She felt closer to her oldest brother through all that was happening, like she finally understood him.

Duty and honor.

"There will not always be walls," Haun said, and Fen wondered at his meaning. Before she could ask, he pointed at the distant trees, whose spiny leaves pointed to the side. The leaves traveled with the sun, pointing always in its direction. At night, they would fall down, only to rise again on the other side as the sun came with the dawn. "The *Hsi Yang* Forest. We're close."

Fen nodded as Haun went back down to steer the craft. The *Guoh Yuan Hsi Yang* Forest, or *orchard of the setting sun*, truly was a beautiful sight. The sun was low, giving a softer glow to the whole valley. After a few minutes, they slowed as they approached a hill which overlooked the valley they traveled in.

A building was on top of the hill. It was small, but Fen could see enough of it to tell it looked very much like one of the palace buildings. It was somewhat misplaced in the wilderness, the tiled rooftop arching toward heaven as it sat high on a tier. Another building, one more rustic in style, was in the middle of construction, though no one presently worked on it. Boards were piled along the side frame and she could see sections yet to be covered.

Pointing at the long building that she was staring at, Haun said, "That will be the school Francesca is starting."

"Is that where they live?" Fen asked, motioning toward the imperial palace-looking structure. She was oddly jealous of Jin and Francesca because they got to live amongst such beauty.

"*Shi*," Haun answered, turning the land craft so they approached the house along the side.

As they neared, Fen saw a figure in black standing before three rows of students. There looked to be about two dozen total. They were doing martial arts exercises.

Fen was jealous of Francesca's talent as well. Though she could defend herself, Fen would never have that woman's capacity for martial arts and self-defense. Glancing back the way they'd come, she was unable to see any sign of the palace. Fen was torn. Part of her really wanted to go back and another part of her wanted to stay on the land craft and keep sailing.

"I should get my disguise," Fen said, glancing around for her cloak.

"Don't bother," Haun answered, slowing them even more. Francesca saw them and waved the children away from her. They ran in the opposite direction, away from the house. "The children will not know you and there are no others here. Francesca has refused to hire servants or guards."

Okay, now that thought was a little frightening. How did Jin do it? They'd been surrounded by people and guards their whole lives. How did he live in such quiet solitude? Didn't he get scared?

"I can't believe our mother agreed to let Francesca live without servants."

"The empress doesn't know." Haun laughed.

"Ah, then...?"

"No. She doesn't know it's just the five of us." Haun didn't look at her as he pulled the craft to a stop.,

"Five?" Fen asked. "Is Francesca pregnant?"

Haun's mouth opened but no sound came out.

"Not that anyone knows of," Francesca said, coming from around the side of the tall house. Her wavy dark brown hair was pulled back from her face, tangled into a mess of curls on top of her head. She had green eyes and strong features.

"Not yet," Jin corrected, walking behind her. Her brother was handsome, like all her brothers, but his hair was longer than she remembered and he looked happier. His shirt was simple, more suited to a middle-class businessman than a prince. The loose-fitting material of both shirt and breeches suited him. He looked relaxed.

"You sound like your mother," Francesca teased through gritted teeth.

Jin held out his hands, coming down the stairs. "Fen, Haun, I'm so glad you're here."

Fen hugged her brother. "What's this about another guest? Do you have someone staying with you?"

"Oh, ah, one of the children is living with us for a short time," Francesca said. "He doesn't have any family."

"Oh, and where are the children? They're not all staying here?" Fen asked, motioning to where Francesca had been training them.

"The rest live in the nearby village of *Tan jau dern.* I sent them home for the night."

Fen knew her sister-by-marriage was an orphan and the news she took care of many children didn't surprise her.

"Come in, food is almost ready," Jin said.

Having seen Francesca out training the children, she asked in surprise, "You cooked?"

"I bought a food simulator," Francesca explained. "It does all the cooking. So technically, food is always almost ready. And before you get alarmed by the metal things crawling around the floor, they're cleaning droids, not an invading threat from space pirates."

"Hey," Jin said, stopping to point at her. "That happened *one* time. It was late, and you didn't tell me you had bought the cleaning droids."

"Yeah," Francesca said sarcastically. "Like I was really going to do all the cooking and cleaning for your lazy royal butt."

Fen watched her brother and his wife, envious of what they had in their marriage, even as she was happy for them. She thought of Shing. He would never be without servants.

Ugh, why did she have to pick his name?

Well, who else would she have chosen?

"Fen?" Francesca asked.

Fen blinked, seeing her brothers disappear inside the house.

"Are you all right?" Francesca asked. "You spaced for a second."

"Mm-hmm," Fen nodded. "Yeah, I'm fine."

"Yeah, that was convincing," Francesca drawled sarcastically. She hooked Fen's arm in hers and pulled, "All right, come for a walk with me."

"But the house..." Fen tried to motion toward the front door.

"I'll give you a tour later." Francesca made her

walk beside her toward a higher part of the hill. "It'll wait. Jin tells me you need a woman to talk to. Why he thinks I'll fit the role, I have no idea, but since Mei's gone, I'm all you apparently have. So shoot."

"Shoot what?" Fen looked around.

"It means speak," Francesca explained with a small laugh. "I've met your mother. I doubt she'd let you come here for a visit without a full entourage unless she had no choice. I know that the emperor has final say, but a woman can always control a man. Not to mention that your brothers are worried about you. They said you've engaged yourself twice? Believe me, I understand wanting to escape the palace, but marriage isn't the answer."

"My escape is not the reason," Fen said softly. She didn't meet her sister-by-marriage's eyes as she looked over the valley below. From the height, the roofs of the nearby village showed. Fen looked for the children running home but couldn't see them. It was getting late and the sun radiated off the surrounding landscape with an orange-red glow. Mist rose from the ground, shadowing the yellow grasses with a light fog.

"Let me guess. The empress caught you in a compromising position and then blackmailed you into marriage by threatening something you hold dear." Francesca arched a brow.

Fen gaped at her in surprise. How could she possibly know that?

"I spent most of my adult life learning how to read people, but in this case, it's pretty simple to see."

"Why?" Fen asked, surprised that Francesca was making her feel better. "Because I'm easy to read?"

"No," Francesca glanced over her shoulder toward the house, "because I scared a confession out of your boyfriend."

"I WANT you to understand something, Piers Aaron," Prince Haun said, placing his hands on Jin's dining table. "Hurt her, and you disappear forever. And I'm not talking being shipped across the Satlyun. I mean gone. Forever."

Prince Jin's home was strangely decorated for a Lintianese prince, with buzzing metallic units rolling along the floor, thick furry rugs and interior doors that all swung open and shut instead of sliding. Outside, it looked just like the building was lifted from the palace. Inside was like stepping into a new universe. Aaron vaguely remembered some of the more rustic furniture elements being like those in his father's home. Considering that Princess Francesca wasn't from their planet, it made sense that she would choose alien elements to decorate her home.

"I understand," Aaron said. After the planned engagement was called off two days before, Aaron hadn't expected much else to come of his fate when it came to Fen. But, somehow, fate had intervened, and he was ordered to be taken away by Prince Haun, only to be dropped off with a note to Prince Jin. He'd been sure he was going to be executed, but instead, he was interrogated about Fen. Once he discovered the brothers and Princess Francesca were concerned over her well-being, and not out to harm him, he'd relaxed. Somehow, they'd guessed his involvement with Fen, but he didn't get the impression it was from Fen herself.

"She's promised herself to Ye Shing," Haun said, "but it's not official."

"We want our sister to be happy," Jin said. "But for her to do that, she needs to enter her marriage with a clean heart. She can't do that if she is pining for you."

Aaron knew what they wanted from him before they even said it. Foolishly, part of him had hoped that the princes were on his side, since Jin was married to Francesca. The woman obviously wasn't born royalty. Was that why they lived out of the palace? Was Jin's wife unacceptable? There was much speculation among the common folk as to why the two had left the palace walls.

"You are asking me to end it with her," Aaron said. He closed his eyes, suddenly very tired. First, he wasn't good enough to be in his own family, and now he wasn't good enough to love Fen. The worst part was he couldn't do anything to change the circumstance of his birth. No matter how hard he worked, how much he learned, he'd still be who he was at this moment—unworthy. "I understand."

"Fen chose her path," Haun said. "And she must walk it. She knows her duty to her family."

"*Shi.*" Aaron nodded once, a hard, curt movement. It was all he could manage.

"Aaron?"

Fen's voice fell over his soul like rain, cleansing him even as it flooded his heart. Instantly, he opened his eyes and stood, moving toward the front door of the home. She stood in the entryway, her body silhouetted by a sharp orange. He couldn't see all the details of her face, but the slim outline of her figure was unmistakable. His body responded, stirring naturally toward her. The mass between his thighs became heavy.

"Aaron," she said, her voice softer than before.

"Come on, brother," Jin said behind him. "Let me show you what we have planned for the grounds."

Fen nodded, giving her brothers a small smile as they passed her. Jin touched her shoulder, leaning over to kiss her cheek before leaving. When they were alone, she said, "I didn't think I'd have a chance to speak to you again. I was sure it was goodbye in the library."

"As did I," Aaron admitted.

"Aaron, I'm sorry for all that has happened, but—"

"Shh, no." Shaking his head, he stepped toward her. Her pretty face became clearer as the orange behind her started to dissipate into night. A breeze swept over her, carrying the smell of flowers to him. "I'm not. I'm only sorry you were shamed by me."

"I admit I was upset at first that you didn't tell me of your past, but I came to realize you were never really given a chance." Fen closed the distance, reaching for his cheek only to hesitate and pull back. She stepped past him, looking around the house. "This is a strange home, isn't it?"

"Princess Francesca," Aaron said. "She designed it from the influence of other humanoid cultures. They call this style early lodge."

"That would make sense," Fen agreed.

"Princess—"

"Fen," she interrupted. "You may call me Fen."

He nodded but didn't say her name.

"Who are you, Aaron?" she asked, her eyes burning as she forgot the house and turned to him. "You have a trade in silk, you design clothes, design material for those clothes, you make tapestries, and yet you know of humanoid décor?"

"I am all those things." He longed to hold her; how his arms ached just to touch her, but he kept himself back. Her brothers were right. He would give her peace in her upcoming marriage. He would answer her questions and then he'd walk away from her life, from this entire life, this planet and these people. He'd make his way in space. He wasn't sure what he'd do, but he'd find something.

"How? I want to understand you."

"After I was orphaned, Lady Hsin taught me the silk trade." Aaron paused. It was a gross understatement. She'd forced him into the silk trade, for he had little other choice in the matter, being as he was so young. "Before that, I lived with my Lintianese mother, Genji, and my human father, Randall Aaron Piers—or translated, Piers Randall. My mother wished to learn all she could about my father's culture so she could understand and know his extraordinary ways. She collected downloads and, when she was done with them, she gave them to me as a young child, wishing to fill my head with knowledge. She was fascinated by human culture outside Lintian."

"And how did they meet? Your parents?" Fen gave him a meek smile and he felt his heart flip. She was so beautiful, so delicate, and yet when she touched him it was pure, intense fire.

"It was an arranged marriage."

"Hmm, arranged marriages." She gave a short, unhappy laugh.

"My parents had love, Fen," he said, though it tore at him to give her the encouragement. "You will as well in yours. How could a man not love you?"

Her expression fell. "You know that I must choose again?"

"*Shi.*"

"And do you know who?"

"Ye Shing."

Fen turned her back on him, pacing toward the doorway leading to a dining area, only to turn back around.

"Ask what it is you want to know but have refused to ask of me," he said.

She didn't even pretend not to know what he was speaking of. "Why did your family disown you?"

The words were more painful to hear from her lips than he'd imagined. Telling Fen his shame, laying it bare for her, was one of the hardest things he'd ever done. People did not talk about such things as this. He'd never said the words aloud before. And even as he didn't blame himself in private, telling her, making it known, was difficult.

"Before I was born, Lady Hsin gave her daughter in an arranged marriage to the owner of an outpost that dealt in the silk exports of Lintian."

"Your father," Fen concluded. When he nodded, she gasped. "Lady Hsin is your grandmother?"

"*Shi*." Aaron answered. "She *was* my grandmother."

"What happened?"

"Though arranged, my mother melted my father's heart and they fell in love. It was out of that love that I was born."

"And why did Lady Hsin arrange the marriage? Just for exports?" Fen moved closer. Even as his thoughts became lost in the past, he could still detect her every movement as if it were his own.

"The match assured an alliance, furthering the wealth of Lady Hsin, then widowed and securing her station in life. Lady Hsin had a direct link to market her silk to the rest of the galaxy and my father supplied her with certain luxuries she'd not be able to get on Lintian."

Aaron slowly walked to a thick sofa. He didn't take a seat, as he waited for Fen to follow his lead. She did, sitting in a chair.

Lowering himself, he continued, "My parents were killed in space. Just a random accident on a glider. With no family on my father's side, and me too young to take care of his affairs, the creditors came like pirates to pick apart my family home. In the end, I was sent to live with a grandmother who wasn't happy to see the foreign reminder of her daughter's death. Her son had died as well, leaving my cousin in her care. She already had one child and a daughter-by-marriage to look after and groom to be her heir."

"How awful," she sighed, shaking her head.

"My mother taught me plenty of my father's people, raised me to walk and eat and talk like them, but she never said anything about her own. When I came here, all I knew was the language. I didn't understand Lintianese customs. I didn't even know how to eat with *kuay tzu*. I thought they were like forks and I stabbed my meat with them."

"That's understandable," Fen interjected.

"Not to Lady Hsin, who had dutifully invited others to see me, her orphaned grandchild. I blundered my way through the evening, scared and not really caring or understanding at the time that I was being rude. In a fit of anger, Lady Hsin announced that I was disinherited. That same night, I was moved to servant quarters, and a week later, she put me in the field to help the mulberry crop.

"At first, I was angry, but then I found I liked watching the crops grow. Before I knew it, I was helping with the butterflies, then with the weaving, until I knew every job in the place. She also gave me an education. Years later, Lady Hsin allowed me to run the business, as I know more than anyone about it. When her grandson, Hsin Wang, inherits the land and title, I've been guaranteed my current place."

Aaron stopped talking. Fen had paled. He waited for her rejection of him, but it never came. Slowly, she stood, moving to sit beside him. She slid her small, delicate hand in his and squeezed. Closing his eyes, he bowed his head forward, drinking in the small comfort.

"It's not your fault," she whispered. "Your fate was the pain of others. I know Lady Hsin, and I do not find her to be a cruel woman."

"I never called her cruel," Aaron defended, though why he was defending the old woman was beyond him. It didn't matter now. He couldn't stay on the same planet as Fen, watching her marry another man, knowing that mere miles separated them. Before, when he only fantasized about her, he was one of a million men who saw her and worshiped from afar. But now he was special. He'd tasted her kiss, felt her skin, knew the tight clasp of her sex in orgasm. Those memories did not fade with time.

"It's funny," Fen said.

Aaron looked at her, frowning.

"Well, not funny so much as ironic. If Lady Hsin had not disowned you, you would now be a noble at the palace as one of my suitors."

No. Not funny at all.

A tear came to her eye. "Maybe cruel *is* the right word for her."

Aaron remembered what he'd been brought before her to do. He wasn't supposed to make her cry, he was supposed to give her closure so she could be happy. If he had any hope, any plausible dream to offer her, he would. But princesses couldn't live on dreams. "Don't dwell on what can't be changed."

Fen swiped her tear.

"Ye Shing seems like a fine nobleman," he lied. In

truth, Ye Shing seemed as spoiled and as arrogant as the rest of them.

"He is," she answered.

"I'm sure you'll find happiness."

"I'm sure I will." She didn't sound convinced, but he admired her brave front.

Aaron wished he knew whether the feelings inside him, the instincts were real, or if they were just hopeful pleas from his heart. Since that first spoken word, that first intense look, he felt as if he'd found part of his soul. And now he had to set his soul free.

"Can I have one last night?" she asked, her hand brushing his thigh. "Tell me you will meet me after everyone's gone to sleep. We might never see each other again once I'm called back to the palace. Please, let's just have this one more night."

Against his better judgment, he nodded. How could he refuse her anything?

"Meet me on the *tu di hang*."

He didn't answer.

"Please, Aaron," Fen begged.

"Fen?" Haun called from the door.

"*Shi,* I'm in here," Fen said, standing to put distance between them.

Aaron also stood. Fen met his eyes and he

nodded in agreement to her question. She sighed, nodding back.

"Fen, you should get some rest," Haun said.

Fen glanced at him before being led away. Aaron headed out the door, his eyes finding the land craft before he headed in the opposite direction.

"You're welcome to stay inside," Francesca said as he passed the royal couple. Jin nodded in agreement.

"No, thank you, Princess Francesca," he answered. "The open air suits me just fine."

One word and everything in a single life was changed. Disowned. Lady Hsin's rash actions were now breaking Fen's heart. But, the bittersweet paradox was, if Lady Hsin hadn't disowned Aaron, he wouldn't be the man she now loved and couldn't have.

One night.

Would that ever be enough? One more night to hold him, feel him, hear him. It was enough to make her want to scream.

"I don't want to be a princess anymore," Fen said, crying into the small round pillow Francesca gave her to sleep on. The bed frame was odd, reaching up and curling over her like claws or horns. She waited for it to close in on her like a hand, smashing her in its wooden palm. "Blessed ancestors, I beg of you. Don't make me give him up. Take away my crown but don't make me give him up. I don't want to marry Shing. Why can't I be happy?"

As much as she wanted him, she also refused to do something to disgrace herself or her title—well, at least in her eyes. The empress would surely call planning to meet Aaron for one last night a clear disgrace.

Curse her mother.

Curse the whole world.

Tonight, she would take one thing for herself. She would treasure every second she could squeeze in with Aaron. She'd hold it tight for the years to come. And, after marriage... No, she couldn't think of playing her husband false. To do so seemed wrong, even in her circumstance.

Unable to wait any longer, she stepped out into the long guest hall, tiptoeing through the darkness so she wouldn't be heard. Going to the door, she stopped as she heard movement behind her.

Fen turned to see Francesca sitting in a chair, watching her. Her sister-by-marriage stood and came toward her.

"I wondered how long it would take you to go to

him," she said, patting her arm. "Don't worry, I didn't see a thing."

Fen smiled, reaching to hug the woman. Francesca stiffened at the sudden contact and patted her awkwardly. "You are a true sister. *Xiexie ni.* Thank you."

Francesca pushed her gently. Fen let go of her.

"The Zhang Dynasty has many laws and traditions," Francesca said. "Just remember something, Fen. Laws and traditions are not such until they are made to be. Before them there was nothing, and given enough time, there will be nothing again."

Fen frowned, confused. Francesca looked sorry for her as she patted her shoulder. Then, with warrior-like grace, her sister-by-marriage disappeared down the hall toward the bedroom she shared with Jin.

The night was cool, fragranced with the smell of trees and flowers. Stars stretched over the distance, blanketing the night sky. In truth, the wide-open space made her uneasy.

The dirt path in front of her brother's house gave way to grass and she stepped through the tickling blades, quickly walking straight for the land craft. It hovered over the ground and she lifted her hand to the eye. Silently, wooden stairs unfolded, falling down to the earth so she could climb aboard. Glancing around the deck, she felt a wave of relief hit her to find that Aaron was already there, waiting for her.

He lay on his back on the upper platform, staring at the stars. Fen leaned over the side, running her hand over the sensor in the eye to pull up the steps. The *tu di hang* again lifted off the ground. Aaron glanced at her, his dark blue eyes shaded by the night, but she knew he looked by the angle of his head. She wasn't sure how he managed to get on board without being programmed into the craft's database, but she was glad he did so she wouldn't have to wait outside in the darkness alone. She ran her hand near the helm, getting the sensors to shut off so the craft wasn't on.

"I had this fear that you wouldn't be here," she said, climbing the few steps it took to get to him. "I was afraid you'd run away."

"I started to," he admitted. "Sometimes I think it would be best if I left and never saw you again."

"You don't wish to be here?" Fen knelt beside his leg, letting her thigh brush his.

"I shouldn't be here. You're to be married. We've both been ordered not to be together, by both of your parents."

"I'm not engaged yet. I haven't asked Shing and I've made him no promises," she answered.

"Why are you marrying him?" Aaron rolled up, sitting so he was facing her. When she didn't speak, he said, "I answered your questions, Fen. Please, I need to know why. You come here with me, but you go to marry him. Why?"

"Because I must." She wanted to leave it at that, but knowing he'd shared so much with her, made her continue. "Because if I don't, you will be given in servitude to Lord He. Because the empress wants me married to a man of Lintianese blood who will give her lots of grandchildren and ensure I never take off like my sister, Mei. And I suspect there is some concern as to our relations with the Song Dynasty, which I'm not being told about, that makes them want to see me settled with a man of power and wealth should anything happen."

"Then why are you here? If they're so urgent to see it done?"

"They think someone is trying to hurt me." This was not how she'd pictured this night going. Emotions flooded her and she began talking nonstop, telling him about the fire the first time they met, of the water, the metal shard, and then finally the wooden stick from Madame Eng's *Chien Tung* set.

"It's believed that whoever is doing it is using the elements through a supernatural force to try and do me harm. Both the astrologers and my ancestors believed that I needed to leave the palace to be safe, so we came out here. I've tried telling myself that it's nothing, that I've been clumsy or unlucky, but in truth I'm terrified."

Her breath caught, and she leaned forward. Aaron pulled her close to his chest, folding his arms around her. She drew strength from his nearness, but that didn't stop tears from rolling down her cheeks. Taking her face in hand, he kissed her, his touch gentle and easy, as he wiped the tears away. Fen needed more.

She pushed him down, riding him to the deck with her mouth firmly planted on his. Her body fit against him, nestling perfectly as if she were carved to be there. Only in these stolen moments did everything make complete and perfect sense.

She pulled at his clothes, eager to have nothing between them, nearly tearing his silk tunic in her haste. Bold hands stroked her hips, rubbing them, drawing her heated sex tight against his arousal. Fen moaned, wiggling as she braced her hand on the deck and reached down with the other to pull her gown around her waist. Aaron flipped her onto her back, kissing a hot trail over the silk bodice of her gown to her exposed stomach. A small sound of pleasure escaped her, and she spread her thighs wide. Aaron drew his mouth along her clit, sucking and biting as he made love to her with his mouth. Soon his hands joined in, his fingers thrusting up into her.

"Fen." Her name came from him in a long moan.

Fen's body jerked as he grabbed her hips, moving her against him. Wanting to feel him inside her, she pulled his hair to get him to slide up her body. He did, only to cradle her close as he flipped onto his back.

Their bodies became a frenzy of movements, hands gliding, hearts pounding, flesh grinding. Clothes were stripped away, pushed aside without thought. Starlight added a soft glow to their skin. Aaron massaged her breasts, pinching the nipples. Fen touched him everywhere she could reach.

She straddled his hips, lifting up only to guide his cock to the apex of her thighs. Closing her eyes, she lowered her body onto his, savoring each stroke of their flesh. He arched his back, groaning in pleasure. She sat astride him, passionately riding him hard and deep. The man without a doubt knew how to move. He reached for the pearl hidden in her slick folds, rubbing it in small circles.

"Mmm, *shi*." She clawed his chest, using it for support as she bucked her hips. Her body built toward a climax.

The orgasm that hit her was intense, taking over her entire length. His finger continued to stimulate her until her clit became so sensitive she thought she'd pass out from pleasure if he kept touching her there. He slowed and she came down for the briefest of seconds. Aaron then built her right back up, making her come a second time. Suddenly, his release joined hers, punctuated by their labored grunts of pleasure.

Fen's body was numb, her bones feeling as if they'd melted right out of her skin. Weak, she collapsed against him, breathing heavily. She didn't want to move.

FEN SLOWLY PULLED off Aaron's unmoving body. He moaned softly but didn't wake back up. They'd rested in each other's arms, talking about nothing and everything, only to make love again. After the second time, they held each other in silence. The stars were bright and beautiful, but as each second passed, she felt more desperate for it never to end.

And then, her body sated and her mind near sleep, she understood what Francesca had been trying to tell her about the laws. They were bendable, breakable even, if done for the right reason. Not all laws were good.

Creeping down the steps, she turned the sensors back on. The land craft lifted ever so slightly, silently ready to move. Fen took a deep breath, and without really thinking of where she was heading, she programmed the *tu di hang* to sail in the opposite direction of the palace.

Wherever they ended up, whatever happened, she wouldn't be scared because she'd have Aaron.

Aaron opened his eyes, stretching his arms over his head. For a brief moment, his mind was clear, his body relaxed from sex and sleep, and he felt a deep peace inside his usually troubled soul. But, as his eyes focused to see the sky and he felt the gentle movements beneath him, his inner peace was replaced by anxiety.

He was on the *tu di hang* with Princess Fen, that much he remembered. Looking around, he was surprised to see Fen at the large wheel. She wasn't touching it, as the craft steered itself. Sitting up, he saw that no one else was on the land craft with them.

What was going on? Where was she taking them?

Fen was dressed in the gown she'd come to him

in. For a brief moment, he let the brilliant image of her burn into his mind. Sunrise cast her in a beautiful glow, shining off her long hair as it blew in the breeze to the side. Before he could stop himself, he whispered her name, "Fen," and she turned. Strands of her hair blew across her face, outlining her eyes. As she ran a finger over her cheek, pulling them off, a slight smile came to her.

Aaron's heart nearly stopped. He was naked but didn't care as he stood to face her. Climbing down the steps, he asked, "Fen?"

"Good morning." She met him halfway and reached up to wrap her arms around his neck. Her lips pursed together and he couldn't resist giving her the kiss she wanted.

He pulled back as he felt himself becoming aroused. "What's going on?"

"I'm kidnapping you," she said, moving to kiss him once more.

Aaron leaned back. "What are you talking about?"

"We're running away," she said.

For a second, his heart soared. Even so, he knew it couldn't be. He let go of her, putting distance between them as he looked for his clothes. "Fen, you can't mean that. Where will we go? What will we do? How will we live?"

"Does it matter?" she asked.

He frowned as he tugged on his pants. "Have you ever gone without a meal?"

"No." The word was hesitant.

"And have you ever washed your own clothes, grown or prepared food? Lived without guards or servants?"

"I'm not a pampered princess," she said defensively, only to shake her head and point at him. "Okay, so I'm a little bit pampered, but I'm not afraid to learn differently. I made my decision. I love you and I want to be with you."

"You're tired and you're not thinking straight." Aaron wished there was a way her plan would work, but he couldn't do it. He jerked on his pants. "You haven't thought this through. Turn the land craft around before it's too late and they realize we've gone."

"You don't want to be with me?" Tears entered her eyes and she looked at him in confusion.

"I can't take care of you," Aaron said. "I don't have the means to support you as you deserve. And that is if we even get away. Princesses aren't exactly easy to hide, you know. Your parents will come after us with every bit of their fortune and every resource at their disposal. Eventually they will find us."

"Why won't you answer? Do you want to be with me?" Fen asked. She put her hands on her hips, looking beautifully defiant and vulnerable at the same time.

Aaron threw his hands to his sides and yelled, "Of course I want to be with you. I can think of nothing else. I dream about you, about us. I think about you all the time. You're in my blood and you drive me mad with passion. I want nothing more than to be with you for the rest of our days, but it can't be. You are a princess and I am a disowned commoner, a peasant."

"I don't care what you are," she whispered.

"But the world does." He motioned around them. "They care very much."

"Then we'll find a new world, like my sister Mei. We'll leave this planet and—"

Aaron held up his hand to stop her. "I've seen your face when you are with your brothers. I cannot take that from you. I will not see your body whither because I don't have the means to feed you. I will not see you sold off at some space auction because I was unable to protect you. The world up there is not like here. There are things that can happen to a beautiful woman that you can't even imagine."

"I'll take that chance. I have to take that chance. Please, Aaron. Let's at least try."

He shook his head in denial. "I love you too much to be with you, Fen, because I know what being with me will mean for you."

A tear slipped over her cheek.

"Don't," he whispered. "Please, don't cry."

"But it's not fair. I've given my whole life to being a princess. I've done the ceremonies, I've served my father's guests. Why can't I have one thing for me?" She collapsed on the deck. The craft kept sailing.

Aaron crossed to her, sinking to his knees. "Fen, we need to turn around and take you back to Prince Jin's. Your brothers will be worried about you. They love you very much. Once you've had a moment, you'll realize this is for the best. Like it or not, you are a princess. Not just in title but in spirit. It's in you, Fen. Think of the years of good you have ahead of you. Think of the difference you can make in the lives of others. If you leave with me, you will come to regret the decision, and I fear that regret will tarnish whatever love you carry. You will begin to miss your family, your home, your honor. I will not see your life or your honor tarnished, nor the honor of your family, nor the whole dynasty, for the sake of my heart."

She sniffed loudly, not answering.

"Fen, please, turn around. Even if we do leave, it won't work. The palace guards will hunt us down. Do you think there is anywhere we could go? Any way we could contact your sister even if we wanted to? And if not for you, think of what they will do when they catch *me*. If the empress was willing to force your hand just to be rid of me, what do you think she'll do to me for kidnapping you?"

"I kidnapped *you*," she defended.

"A small point in their eyes," he assured her. In some ways she was so smart, but in others, she was very naive. The same rules did not apply to his class that did hers.

"Then what would you have me do?" she asked, her voice weak.

"I would have you stand up, turn us around, and face your duty like the princess you were born to be." Aaron waited for a long moment. "The rest is up to fate. But, if you marry, know that I want you to be happy. I want you to love, bear children and spare me a kind thought when the moment allows it. But know always that I love you, and if you ever have need of me, I am eternally at your service."

Fen nodded, pushing on his shoulder to stand. He patted her hand briefly before she turned to reprogram the land craft.

Inside, his heart screamed at the agony, but the princes had been right. Aaron needed to give Fen closure. He needed to make it easier on her to face what she must. Though it tore at him to think of her loving another, he wished it for her sake. He wished her delight in all things. Above all else, he would see her happy.

The *tu di hang* slowed, turning around to head back in the other direction. The sun rose higher and Aaron feared they wouldn't make it back before her brothers awoke. The land craft picked up speed, gliding over the gentle rolling hills of the prairie, along the tree line of the *Hsi Yang* Forest.

"Hold me," Fen said, standing next to him. "Just until we get back."

Aaron held her tight against his chest. They didn't speak as they crossed the distance. The thought that she'd been willing to give up everything for him astounded and saddened him. His heart soared that she could love him that much, and yet it died in the same moment, for it could never be.

FEN SAW the outline of Jin's house approaching in the distance. It was early morning yet, but she saw the figures of her brothers and Francesca outlined in the sky. Aaron let go of her, putting distance between them. He stood rigid, his face blank and hard. She hated him for being right, for making her turn back. She hadn't been thinking, but as the day cleared and her thoughts centered with her logic, she knew this was the course of action they must take.

But if he said the word, she'd turn the land craft around in a second and race away with him to meet their impoverished fate. She looked at him, expectant, hoping. The words never came.

"Fen," Haun yelled. He sounded angry. Swallowing, she turned to look at him as the ship approached where he stood. He *was* angry.

"I just—" Fen began.

"Save the excuses," Haun growled. The ship neared, and he lifted his hand to the eye, bringing down the stairs. Fen moved past Aaron to step down. Haun reached up and grabbed her hand, tugging her toward him. She tripped.

"Easy," Aaron said as he grabbed her waist from behind, holding her up. For a moment, she teetered between the land craft and the ground.

"What?" Haun's voice was hard. She knew he was worried, which translated into anger.

"Haun," Jin said, his voice softer. "She's safe. She's all right. You can let go."

"She's a fool," Haun answered. He let go of her, prompting Aaron to do the same. Fen quickly stepped down, moving to block Aaron from Haun's view.

"Haun, I'm sorry. I'm here now." Fen lifted her hand, but his glare stopped her.

"I was charged with your safety, Fen. What would have happened if you didn't come back?"

"I did," she answered. She was mildly surprised that he knew she'd planned on running away, but she shouldn't have been.

"And you," Haun said, lifting his hand. "I warned you to mind yourself."

Fen glanced at Aaron. He tried to give her a reassuring half smile but it didn't hold.

"It was me," Fen said. "I needed to clear my head. I did that, and now I'm ready to go home."

"But you can't," Jin protested. "You just got here, and what about the threat?"

"Maybe we could take a trip to the palace with you," Francesca offered, taking her husband's arm.

Fen nodded in silent thanks.

"You could've ruined everything," Haun said.

Unable to take his accusing tone, not now when her heart was broken and she was forced to make the hardest decision of her life—leaving Aaron—she screamed.

Haun and Jin looked shocked. Francesca grinned, nodding in approval. Aaron didn't move.

"I am tired of you all telling me what to do," she yelled. Pointing at Aaron, she said, "I know my duty, and I am doing it." She moved her finger, directing her attention at Haun. "And I'll marry Li or Shing or whoever our royal dictator of a mother decides to put next to me, and I'll be a puppet wife." She moved her finger toward Jin. "I know my life is in danger. I more than anyone know it. *Shi*, someone wants me dead.

Shi, it's dangerous. *Shi*, I know I was told to get away from the palace. Well, I'm away, and now I'm going back. No one said how long I had to stay away." Then, turning to Francesca, she hesitated, stuttering, "Ah, I—I am not really mad at you so...there!"

"What are you saying, Fen?" Haun asked.

"She's saying," Francesca interrupted, "that she's fed up, and you men really suck ass right now. Quit treating her like she's a baby, when it's clear she's doing what she has to like an adult. Hell, I practically told her to run away. So what if she tried it; she came back, didn't she? Actually, right now, I'm a little pissed at you myself. Am I the only one who thinks forcing someone to marry is wrong?" She paused to look at Jin. "Not counting us, my love." Jin nodded, a small smile on his face as he watched his wife.

Fen crossed over to Francesca, grateful to have someone understanding on her side. She stood beside the woman, nodding her head in agreement with her sister-by-marriage's words, as she silently thought, *Go, sister, go.*

"Fen and I are going back to the palace just as soon as I pack," Francesca announced. She turned to Fen. "You have clothes I can borrow? I don't have suitable princess attire. I keep avoiding the seamstresses your mother sends."

They weren't the same size, but Fen nodded that she did.

"Great." Francesca then turned to the men. "As I said, Fen and I are going back right now. You can either get on board, or stay here, but one thing is for sure—Aaron, you had better get your ass on that land craft before I tie you up and drag you back to the palace as my prisoner."

"Um, she can do it," Jin warned.

"Thanks, sweetheart," Francesca said to him.

"Ah, yeah, what she said," Fen told Haun and Jin.

Haun lifted up his hands. "Well, do you at least have a plan?"

"Francesca already told you," Fen said. "We're going back to the palace."

"I meant beyond that?" he asked, his tone not so angry as before. He gave her a quick hug before stepping away from the rampaging Francesca.

"I don't know," Francesca said, giving Fen a mischievous look. "Lunch maybe?"

"Perfect," Fen said, leading the way back up the steps. Francesca was right behind her.

"I meant about the threat on Fen's life," Haun stepped up.

"Honey," Francesca told her brother-by-marriage. "Life and death situations are my department of expertise. I'll be by her side until the scoundrel is caught, then I'll neuter him through his nose for daring to threaten my sister."

The men winced, each protectively adjusting their bodies.

"I've been itching for a little action," Francesca said, almost sounding excited. Fen guessed that living the married life was a lot tamer than the existence of the intergalactic thief she'd once been. To Fen, Francesca whispered, "Don't worry about a thing. If you love him so much that you were willing to give up your crown for him—and I know how you all prize family and honor on this planet—then I'll help you find a way to be with him. If there isn't already a way around the law, then we'll just have to change a few things so there is."

"How do you know I was the one who was willing to leave? How do you know I didn't make him come back?" Fen asked, awed by Francesca's deep, almost psychic assessment of the situation.

"I can read people. He wouldn't dare kidnap you, because you have everything to lose. Just look at his eyes when he's staring at you. He would roll over and die if you told him to do it. I just can't believe he convinced you to come back. I rather thought you'd sneak off, get married and *then* come back. But this plan works too." Francesca shrugged, crossing over to the controls. She hit the preset coordinates for the palace.

"Thank you," Fen said, placing her hand on her shoulder.

"Fen, you were a true friend to me despite everything I was when we met. You showed me that there was more to marrying Jin than getting a husband. You showed me the love of a sister. Protecting you is the least I can do to repay that kindness."

"I did that?" Fen was surprised, not remembering herself doing anything special. She'd tried to get along with the woman but had always assumed her measures went unappreciated.

Francesca winked at her but didn't change her somber expression. Louder, she announced, "We're going. You'd better be on board if you're coming along."

"*Qin ai de, baobei, ai ren,*" Jin said to his wife, speaking the long list of endearments as if to placate her before daring to question her order that they leave.

"Don't darling, baby, sweetheart me," Francesca told him. "I think it's time we paid your parents a visit. I also think it's time they stopped meddling in their children's lives, especially if they want to see their grandchild after it's born."

"What?" Fen gasped. "Francesca?"

"Jin?" Haun asked.

"She just told me," Jin said, nodding.

"A baby?" Fen asked, grinning in excitement. "But you said—"

"I said not that anyone knew," Francesca put forth.

"Oh, my, a baby? Really?" Fen gave a small clap of excitement. She really needed some good news.

"Yes. And since everyone knows that pregnant women have to get their way or risk the baby coming out with two heads..." Francesca smiled as her voice tapered off.

Fen stared at her in amazement. Then, seeing Aaron standing quietly behind her brothers, atop the platform where they'd made love the night before, she tried to smile at him in hope. He nodded once, returning the look. Fen couldn't blame him for not speaking, and knew he'd feel it wasn't his place since he was the only non-member of the family.

"Uh, Jin," Haun said, uncertain. "Foreign women don't really have babies with heads like that, do they?"

"No." Jin chuckled. "You were teasing, right, *ai ren?*"

Francesca just smiled.

Fen shook her head. Her poor brothers really didn't have a clue when it came to those types of things. Aside from a few servants, they'd probably never even seen a pregnant woman, let alone knew what was natural during such a time.

"Ah, *ai ren?*" Jin asked. "Right?"

Francesca laughed.

"Right, *ai ren?*"

Fᴇɴ's sᴛᴏᴍᴀᴄʜ had tightened into hard knots the second the walls of Honorable City came into view and the feeling didn't ease up in the hours since. Her parents were upset by her return, even more so to see Aaron was with her. Jin stole Aaron away, saving him from the scrutiny of the emperor and empress. Haun left to speak to their father, and Francesca somehow managed to turn the conversation in so many directions until the empress all but made them go to Fen's room to rest. Since that was originally what Francesca wanted, they were hardly disappointed.

"I don't know if I'm strong enough to go through with this," Fen said, taking a deep breath as she thought about the plan they'd come up with on the ride home. She smoothed the black silk of her gown. Delicately embroidered red blossoms on a stem wound around the black silk. She'd bathed in the decontaminator, and then had taken time to pull up her hair with a black comb. "I'm not like you."

"Yes, you are," Francesca said. As her figure was more athletic in build, Fen's dresses didn't fit her so well, so she'd gone to Jin's room to steal a pair of his breeches and combined it with one of Fen's plain nightshirts. After tying a belt around her waist, it didn't look half bad. "You just haven't had the occasion to tap into your inner strength. It took a lot of guts to try and run away from everything you'd been taught."

"I don't see it as guts. I see it as being a coward and not facing what I must," Fen said.

"Are you serious? With the way honor and duty have been drummed into your head... Now, don't take this the wrong way, I agree that those are good qualities to have, but to give up everything you hold dear, to give up the chance at love because you feel you are honor bound to marry a man who was born under the right circumstances? When I think that Jin and I..." Francesca paused, touching her stomach. "When I think that we might not have all we do now because I'm not Lintianese..."

Fen saw a tear enter Francesca's eye, but the woman quickly blinked it away.

"Your parents love you," Francesca said. "Your mother is a piece of work, but she's still your mother. If she can deal with Mei and Jarek and Jin and me, then she'll be fine with what you have planned. Besides, if she disowns you, you can always come live with me. I need a good servant."

Fen laughed, despite her nervousness. "Don't you think I should talk to Aaron first?"

"Ah, yeah, about that. You can't. Your mother has him under guard. Jin told me when I went to get the pants." Francesca patted her arm. "But don't worry, he's unharmed. Just...under arrest."

"Just?" Fen shook her head in disbelief at the easy way Francesca said it, as if it was no big deal to be arrested by the emperor.

"Hey, I was in your prisons," Francesca said. "They're not bad at all. He'll be fed, given a place to sleep. As far as prison holds go, I have to say it's the best one I've been in. By stars, it's better than some of the rooms I've paid good space credits to stay in. If word got out, people would come here just to get arrested."

"I think it's time," Fen said. "They're expecting us in the dining hall. All the suitors will be there."

"Don't worry, I'll be by your side the whole time," Francesca said. "No one is going to hurt you."

"Strangely, at the moment, I'm less concerned about being attacked than facing the empress."

"Nothing strange about it." Francesca hooked her arm through Fen's and began walking toward the door. "I'd much rather get in a fight than face your mother in defiance."

"Somehow, that doesn't make me feel a whole lot better."

"I've seated Shing at your side," the empress said, joining Fen and Francesca as they came through the door. "He is ready to accept your hand in marriage. It has all been arranged, there is nothing to discuss with him."

"You asked him for me?" Fen gasped. Her gaze flew to the table. Her suitors were there, including some of the new ones. Deng Li was gone, but that wasn't too surprising, as he didn't have any need to stay at the palace and could get back to his life. Seeing Shing talking with Tan Ho, she shivered. He was handsome, refined and not the person she wanted to spend the rest of her life next to.

"*Shi*," the empress said.

"That's romantic," Francesca drawled wryly.

The empress shot her a hard look but otherwise didn't acknowledge the comment.

"The astrologers are on their way. I've spoken to Madame Eng, and she assures me that there should not be any reason to call the nuptials off. I had her do the readings in private. As soon as you announce, they'll give their verdict agreeing to the match." The empress smiled for any eyes that might be looking, but her gaze was hard. "I expect this to go smoothly."

The empress walked away, not giving her time to answer.

"*Tianna*," Fen whispered to Francesca when they could again speak freely. "She's already engaged me. I can't get out of it now. They've given my word on the matter."

"Only *you* can give your word," Francesca argued.

"There is obviously more you need to learn about our culture," Fen whispered. Her heart pounded in her chest. She couldn't do it. She wasn't strong enough to stand up to society and her parents. What if they disowned her? What if they had no choice but to? What if Shing protested and demanded compensation for refusing their engagement? She had to go through with it. Why did she even think she could get out of it?

"Princess Fen."

Fen turned to see Ye Yuan. His gaze was downcast and dark circles marred under his eyes. The man was usually brooding, but there was something else to his forlorn expression.

"Please, may I speak?" Yuan asked, giving the barest glance at Francesca.

Fen motioned that it was all right and Francesca made her way toward the dining table where people were being seated. When they were relatively alone, Fen turned expectantly to Yuan, ready to hear his well wishes on her marriage to his brother, and perhaps a brief welcome into their family. She bit her lips, feeling nauseous.

"You, ah..." Yuan glanced around the hall before again giving her his full attention. "Princess, you can't marry my brother."

That was the last thing she'd suspected. "Excuse me?"

"You can't marry Shing. You're not meant for him. Please, you can't marry him. If you must, marry me instead, but not Shing. He'll... I'll..."

Fen frowned. Something in the man's eyes scared her. The hairs on the back of her neck stood up in warning.

"Ah, my beautiful princess," Shing's voice interrupted. He came next to his brother, smiling brightly as he offered Fen his arm. "May I escort you to the table?"

"But—" Yuan began.

"Yuan, you don't look well," Shing said. "Maybe you should go lie down."

"But—" the troubled man said again.

"Come." Shing took Fen's hand and put it on his arm before leading her away.

"Is he...?" Fen glanced back.

"Who, Yuan? Oh, sure, he'll be fine," Shing assured her. "He is a little different. My mother had him tutored partially by a religious sect when he was younger and we think it affected his mind some. He's harmless though. Yuan spends most of his time praying to the ancestors, and what harm can there be in that?"

A cold chill washed over Fen at Shing's words. The fire had been something supernatural. Could it be that Yuan was behind the attacks? The man was brooding and troubled, with a wild look about him. And he'd been almost desperate when he said she should choose to marry him, not Shing.

It all added up—raised by a sect, praying to ancestors excessively, in the shadow of a charming and well liked older brother who was set to inherit land and title, and was now engaged to a princess. But why attack her? Because he didn't want his brother to have her? Her brothers did say that she'd been noticeably spending more time with Shing than the others. Did Yuan notice the same thing as well?

Fen looked back to see Yuan was gone from the hall. Stress kept her entire body on a tight leash, making it hard to breathe. They reached the table and Fen tried to extract her arm from Shing. He held it a bit tighter, leaning into her.

"I am pleased with this," he said, his eyes intense.

Fen couldn't answer. Her mind raced with thoughts of Yuan. If he was the one, they could stop him, get him help, and she'd be safe. A sense of relief tried to unfurl in her at the idea. How could she not have seen it? But, then, with so many suitors vying for her attention all the time, it was understandable how she hadn't. Her emotions were all over the place and she'd been so focused on Aaron that she hadn't taken time to use her gifts on the suitors.

Shing let go of her hand when she didn't answer and she pulled away from him to take her seat. Fen avoided his eyes, not wanting to see his disappointment. She didn't want to hurt his feelings.

Francesca was near, though not close enough to talk to. Jin was beside her, and Haun beside him, then Shen and Lian. Servants came to deliver the food, but she didn't think she could eat anything. The light murmur of conversation sounded over the table. Shing said something, repeating himself three times, and still his words didn't register.

Time inched along and Fen felt as if she'd been emotionally beat up by the time after-dinner tea was served. The *shui guo cha* blend was a little too spicy, but she forced herself to drink it.

"I can't believe I wasn't informed of this," An's voice came down from above. Fen resisted the urge to look up. "You would think it was enough that I sent the signs to Madame Eng about Deng Li, but now your mother presumes to try this again without first consulting me? I can't believe it. The woman is too much."

Fen stopped moving. Did her great-grandmother just admit to fixing the first marriage proposal?

"You shouldn't be back here," An continued. "I whispered in the astrologers' ears that there was a cold presence in Honorable City. I knew your mother would listen to them, and not to me if I was to warn her. The palace grows colder with each passing day. Some of the ancestors refuse to leave the burial chamber for fear the strange force will exorcise them. I was happy to see you leave until we could figure out who brought the shadow into our home." Fen stiffened as An's face suddenly appeared upside down before hers. She could see through the woman's eyes to look at her parents on the other side. "Are you listening to me?"

"*Shi*," Fen whispered into her cup as she lifted it to her mouth. An was so close that the rim of the cup slipped through her transparent nose. Her great-grandmother's expression wrinkled and pulled away, until Fen could only presume the ancestor once more floated above her head where she couldn't see her. Fen lifted her cup again, saying very quietly. "An, check Ye Yuan. He was acting strange."

"What?" An demanded, her voice carrying.

"Ye Yuan," Fen stressed, trying not to be noticeable.

"What about my brother?" Shing asked.

"Maybe we should send someone to check on him. Make sure he is well," Fen said, weakly. "I'm worried he didn't look in the best of health."

"Oh, you want me to check on Yuan," An said. "Why didn't you just say so?"

Fen sighed.

"I'm sure he's fine," Shing said, dismissing the words. "Let him pout."

"Pout?" Fen asked, catching the word.

"I meant brood," Shing said. That word was little better.

"Shing, there is something I should tell you," Fen said.

"Ah, here come the astrologers, Princess," Shing said, changing the subject and not letting her talk. The empress stood. Fen looked at Francesca. Her sister-by-marriage motioned that she should get up, her eyes steadily telling her to take a stand. Jin glanced at his wife, his brow wrinkled as he leaned in to whisper in Francesca's ear.

Fen didn't stand. Her mother came to her side, expectantly. She was aware of the eyes on her, of those who watched, ready for the match to be proclaimed.

"Fen," the empress ordered in a whisper.

Fen shook her head slightly in denial, trying to find her voice. Did she have the strength to openly defy the woman's will?

The empress made a strange noise. Fen looked at her mother, slowly standing.

"BLESSED ANCESTORS, don't let her marry Shing. Don't let her marry my brother."

Yuan rocked back and forth, repeating the same words over and over in desperation. An watched him from above, frowning at the way he clutched his arms and mumbled the nearly incoherent words. Her eyes widened to see the candles set up on the low makeshift altar in the guest room. It was simple, easily covered by shoving it under the bed. That must have been why she didn't see it before as she'd glided through the rooms to see Fen's intended.

Fading, she sped toward the hall. The emperor needed to know the trouble that stirred within the palace walls. It was more serious than she'd first thought, for this was no natural force that Yuan's altar was set up to receive, and it was no ancestor that would hear his call for help.

No, Yuan called to something much older and much darker—an ancient power that had lived on Lintian long before they'd arrived. Some of the first settlers had discovered the tomb in a cave, had learned to work the magic for themselves. The cave had been destroyed and all the followers were to have been killed.

If Yaun was trained at all in what he was doing, it might already be too late to stop the force that he called upon her great-granddaughter.

AARON CLOSED HIS EYES, hating the empress for ordering him to watch Fen engage herself yet again to another nobleman. He was hidden in the corner, concealed by darkness but able to see. The dinner seemed to last forever. He noticed Fen didn't eat.

He cursed himself for making her turn the land craft back, even though he knew that wasn't the life he would ask of her. When the man, Shing, touched her, Aaron felt a deep heat rise up inside him. He wanted to fight, to scream, but what good would that do him? He'd only embarrass Fen and injure himself as the palace guards came tumbling down upon him to make him stop.

Blessed ancestors, he prayed, *make her happy. No*

matter what happens to me, let her be blessed with a long and happy life.

When he again opened his eyes, it was to see Fen standing. She was beautiful in the dark silk, just as he knew she would be when they'd picked out the dress design together. The gown must have been finished by Lady Hsin's workers the night before because he didn't remember seeing the final garment.

Fen stood as the empress called forth the astrologers. The old women in green came forward, holding their mystical items ready.

"Madame Eng," the empress said. The hall was quiet. Aaron stared at Fen. She didn't move. "It is the wish of my daughter to—"

Fen put her hand on her mother's arm. Aaron stood a little taller.

"It is my wish to marry," Fen said, lifting her chin. Shing stepped forward behind her.

Aaron felt his heart stop beating. He couldn't do it. He had to say something.

"Many blessings," Madame Eng said. Her words were followed by the exact same phrase being repeated in unison by the other astrologers.

"It is my wish to marry—" Fen repeated.

"No," Aaron yelled, stepping forward into the light. "Fen, no, you can't!"

Just as he said the words in protest, Fen said, "Piers Aaron."

Aaron stopped. Fen smiled at him. The empress gasped, and the suitors stood from their chairs. Only the emperor remained seated.

"Aaron," Fen said, moving to come to him.

"Princess," Shing said, reaching to stop her.

"Fen," the empress scolded.

"*Bi zui*," Fen growled. Aaron was proud of her. It was clear by the empress' face that her children never told her to shut her mouth. "I said I wish to marry Piers Aaron."

Fen's heart filled to hear Aaron's defiance. She knew what it took for him to speak up like he did, just as she knew he thought his silence was the best thing for her.

"Whoo-hoo, Fen," Francesca yelled, clapping. She was the only one in the hall showing such enthusiasm. The empress groaned at the sound but didn't bother to correct her daughter-by-marriage. They all knew Francesca did things on her own terms and wouldn't be controlled. Fen was glad. She smiled at the woman, nodding her thanks.

Her brothers grinned at her, all but Haun, who slowly nodded his head in approval.

"Please tell us if it is to be a blessed and happy match," Fen commanded the astrologers when they didn't readily offer their blessing on her choice. "And mind you, I call forth my ancestors to verify the accuracy of the reading."

"We would never read false," Madame Eng said in affront.

"It would be a great honor, Princess," Madame Cong inserted, pulling Madame Eng back.

"A true honor," Madame Bing assured her, raising her hand as if to pat her calmingly through the air.

"Fen," Shing said, his face red in upset.

"Shing, I'm sorry, but I don't love you," Fen said. "The empress should not have spoken on my behalf. I do not ask you to marry me."

"But..." Shing shook his head, storming from the hall the way his brother had left.

Fen looked at the astrologers as she crossed the floor toward Aaron. "If you would, please, Madame Eng."

Aaron met her halfway, crushing her to his chest. It felt right being in his arms, good to be held by him for all to see. She knew her mother was angry, and it hurt that the woman couldn't be happy for her, but this is what she wanted. Aaron was who she needed. Without him, she wouldn't be whole, and she had every confidence that the astrologers would discover the same when they read their future together.

"It'll take time," Madame Eng said.

"Then you'd better start," Fen answered, not taking her eyes off him. "Otherwise, you'll miss your chance to be in the history scrolls on this one. Because with or without your consent, I will marry him. I'll take my chance with fate."

"I love you, Fen," he said. "I should have fought for you earlier. I'm sorry."

"No, I'm sorry. I should have proclaimed my love for you right from the start, the wishes of others be damned," she said.

"Be damned?" Aaron arched a brow.

"Oh, ah, Francesca." Fen gave a small laugh, as she indicated where she'd gotten the phrase. "She was on a rant earlier."

"It's Yuan!"

Fen blinked, looking around the hall for An. The spirit rushed into the room.

"Everyone, out," the emperor yelled, finally standing from his throne. Her suitors instantly obeyed, silently filing out of the hall. Her family remained. To the astrologers, he said, "Go see to my daughter's choice."

"But we must consult with Pier—" Madame Eng began.

"Then do what you can without him," the emperor ordered. "And get his birth date and such from him later. Now go."

The astrologers bowed, quickly shuffling from the hall.

"Should I—?" Aaron began.

"Grandmother," the emperor said, "show yourself to all."

"Grandmother?" Aaron whispered.

Fen nodded at An. She must've appeared to Aaron, because he stiffened.

"Aaron, this is my great-grandmother, Zhang An," Fen introduced. An nodded her head in distracted acknowledgement as she rushed forward, her body fluttering wildly in her haste.

"Ye Yuan," An said. "He practices *The Ancient Way.*"

"What?" the empress asked in shock.

"You are certain?" the emperor demanded.

"You cannot be listening to her," the empress said. "She is merely trying to distract us from," she paused to wave at Fen and Aaron, "this. She's making it up. She always does this. She meddles—"

"I have had enough," the emperor said. He crossed to his wife. "I understand your heart, but enough. Mei chose her fate. The battle between you and An is finished. I will have no more of it. This is not how family should be."

The empress opened her mouth to protest, but his look stopped her.

"Finished," he repeated. Then to An, he said, "Blessed ancestor, it is finished between you two. No more scheming. I have enough problems with the world without there being problems in my hall."

"I never scheme," An said, looking up and away.

"Finished," the emperor asserted.

An nodded once, her lips tight. "*Shi.* Finished."

"But what of..." The empress motioned to Fen and Aaron.

Fen patted Aaron's arm and pulled away to face her father.

"I love him," Fen said to the emperor. "And I believe if you only talk to him, you will come to love him as a son."

"I agree with Fen's choice," Lian said. "I feel he's best for her."

"As do I," Shen agreed.

"But he is disowned," the empress said between clenched teeth. "A dishonorable man will not... He cannot... Fen..."

"Ask him," Fen told her father. "Please, talk to him. Ask him why, before you judge him for it. Ask him who his family is."

"But he's not..." the empress tried again, not sounding as confident since her husband's stern announcement.

"What? Noble?" Fen asked. "No, not technically. But by blood, he is the grandson to Lady Hsin. Her family line is as old as any on this planet. If blood is what you are worried about, then make her take back her disownment. Surely, if she was the one to disclaim him, she would be the one to take it back."

"But...?" the empress' lips trembled. "It doesn't work that way."

"There's a first time for everything," Fen declared. "Some laws are just plain stupid."

"Stupid?" the empress repeated.

"*Shi*, stupid," Francesca asserted as she lifted her chin. "You're the Zhang emperor and empress. If you cannot make it so, then who? Besides, if you don't, your daughter will marry a peasant and still be completely and utterly happy, whether you like it or not."

"Jin," the empress warned.

"What? You think my husband can still my tongue? Not in this, Empress," Francesca argued. "Like it or not, we foreigners are diluting your family line."

The empress gasped, her mouth working again but no sound coming out.

"Now, leave Fen alone so she can be happy with the man she obviously loves, or I will never let you see the grandbaby I'm carrying." Francesca folded her arms over her chest.

Jin merely looked at her, smiling like a fool in love. Fen had never seen her brother so relaxed, especially when it came to tradition and honor. Francesca was definitely the best thing that had ever happened to him.

"She's right," Jin said. "All we want is for Fen to be happy."

"I never said I didn't want you to be happy." The empress' voice was a mere whisper as she stared at her daughter. "I've only been thinking of your future happiness." Suddenly, she stopped, turning to Francesca. "You're giving us a baby?"

Francesca nodded. The empress started to smile, shook her head in confusion, and then turned back to the matter at hand.

The emperor sighed. "This all will work itself out. We will see what the astrologers have to say. First, I would have my family safe. Grandmother, what of Ye Yaun? What did you see?"

"He's at an altar in his guest chamber, begging that Fen doesn't marry Shing," An said. "He looks crazed."

Fen reached behind her for Aaron and felt his hand instantly fold into hers. He came next to her back and she drew comfort from his presence.

"Don't worry, I won't let anyone hurt you," Aaron said softly.

The emperor looked at him but said nothing. He turned to An. "Go keep an eye on him."

"What are you going to do?" Fen asked.

"We're going to confront him." As the emperor walked toward the door, his steps were quick and angry. He shouted an order for the guards and instantly three were following behind him.

Fen stayed close to Aaron, her body trembling as she forced her legs to move.

Suddenly, her father stopped. Turning to Aaron, he said, "Keep her here."

Aaron bowed his head. Fen glanced between the two men, then her father continued on, followed by the rest of her family.

"Come, Fen, sit," Aaron urged, leading her to the Hall of Infinite Wisdom's front steps.

"Here?"

"Why not?" he answered. They sat on the steps. Aaron pulled her close to his chest, holding her tight. "They'll get him, don't worry."

"I love you," Fen said, needing him to know. "I meant what I said. Either I'll marry you or no one. I don't love Shing. I can't be happy with him. I won't be happy with anyone but you."

He hugged her tighter and didn't answer. His silence didn't bother her like it had before. She knew he loved her, was willing to risk angering an emperor to prove it, that's all she needed to know. Some things really didn't need to be said.

"I have to see what's happening," Fen said, pulling away.

"Your father told me to keep you here," Aaron protested. "I don't want to disappoint him."

"This is my threat," Fen said. "I need to know."

Aaron hesitated. Fen pulled his hand, leading him toward Péng You Hall. "Tell him I ordered you. No one would expect you to deny a royal princess."

"No, you don't understand," Yuan was yelling at the top of his lungs when they arrived. He was being dragged by two guards. The third guard held pieces of a broken altar in his hands. "I only want what's best for the princess. I can protect her. I love her. She should marry me, not Shing. He's not right for her. Please—"

Fen shivered. Yuan's eyes met hers and he stopped fighting. He was crying. Blood trickled down a deep gash in his arm.

"Please, I'd never hurt you," Yuan said to her. "I swear on my blood, I'd never hurt you."

"Fen." Aaron tried to pull her away.

Fen didn't move as she watched the guards haul Yuan off to the prison hold. She felt sorry for the man, even as she feared the wildness in him.

The emperor eyed her warily as he came to them. To Aaron, he said, "She ordered you, didn't she?"

Fen gave a small laugh and nodded, though she was too shaken up to see much humor in the situation.

"I thought you might, daughter," the Emperor said. "We found Yuan offering a blood sacrifice. He claims he was calling the ancestors, but the ancestors do not respond to blood. What he called forth was much darker in purpose."

"*The Ancient Way?*" Fen asked, frowning. "I thought that was a folktale."

"All folktales are founded by fact," Haun said.

He would know, as he studied all the secret scrolls. Haun and their parents knew more of the secret history of the planet than anyone.

"It came from the species who lived here before us." An floated above them. "They killed themselves off in a frenzy of blood sacrifices, murdering anyone, even family, for the power the killing wrought. It was long before our people arrived. But, some did find the caves that housed these horrific cults and learned to harness the power with our own. They found a way to use their own blood to summon those from the past, evil, bloodthirsty spirits. They called their religion *The Ancient Way*."

"The caves were sealed shut long ago, their location lost with time," the emperor said.

"It would seem someone found them." Jin looked to where Yuan had been dragged off to.

"Shing mentioned Yuan was raised by a religious sect," Fen offered. "If that's true, there may be more of them."

"Father," Haun asserted. "We should question Yuan. If there are more, they'll need to be dealt with. We cannot have this knowledge spreading. It can only lead to our demise."

"I agree," Shen said.

"Me, too," Lian added. "What if someone else

tries to magically hurt one of us? We should stop the problem before it starts."

"Maybe you should let me talk to him," Fen put forth. "If he thinks he loves me, maybe he'll tell me what we what to know."

"Fen, no," Aaron said. "I can't let you do that."

"I'll go with her," Francesca offered.

The emperor held up his hands. "Francesca, your purpose is much more delicate right now. I will not risk a grandchild for this."

Francesca frowned, ready to argue. Jin put his hand on her shoulder and shook his head in denial.

"Fen, I don't like the idea of you going in there, but you may be right," the emperor said. "Haun, take Shen and Lian with you."

"I'm going," Aaron asserted.

The emperor gave a short laugh. "I hardly doubted you'd stay behind."

"And me?" Jin asked.

"See to your wife," the emperor said. "You have your hands full with her."

Francesca giggled, nodding her head in agreement. Jin kissed the tip of her nose and whispered in her ear.

"Now, Fen, listen to me. You have to stay calm.

Don't let him see you getting riled," Haun said. "This isn't like reading an ambassador."

Fen took a deep breath, nodding her head. "I just want this all to be over. I want my life back." She paused, looking at Aaron. "I want my new life to start."

30

"I HAVE DONE everything to make her happy. I have given of myself and still she denies me. And for what? That peasant at her side? She doesn't deserve to live. She deserves to be buried beneath the earth, smothered until all breath is stolen from her body. How could she pick him, blessed ancestors, how? After all my patience. Well, no more. I beg you to kill her, blessed ancestors. Make her pay for what she's done to me. Make her pay for what she's done to my heart. Kill her, blessed ancestors. Kill her."

FEN DOUBTED her bravery as they opened the door to Yuan's cell. The imperial prisons were more like guest rooms, minus the freedom. A bed was on one side, a small decontaminator on the other. The walls were bare, but there was a silk coverlet on the bed.

Yuan looked up at her as she entered, his eyes wild as he rocked back and forth. One of his wrists had been chained to a bedpost, giving him enough room to get on and off the bed but not go much farther.

"Ye Yuan," Fen said, comforted by the fact that her brothers were beside her. Aaron lightly touched her back behind her, though he didn't openly make a move to show affection. They didn't want to upset Yuan any further than he already was.

"I know why you're here," the prisoner said, laughing, a cold, cackling sound. "I know, I know, they told me."

"Who told you?" Haun asked.

He glared at the man, refusing to answer.

"Who?" Fen kept her voice gentle and dared a step forward.

"They," he answered.

"Yuan, can you tell us about them? Where did you first see them?" Fen asked. When he tried to look away, she tilted her head to keep his eyes on hers. "Are there more who see them?"

"*Shi*," he answered, nodding.

"Do they want to hurt me, Yuan?" Fen asked.

"I only meant to protect you," he said.

"I know that," Fen lied, doing her best to remain calm and even-toned. "I know."

"I failed," he said.

"How? How did you fail?" She took a step closer, sensing he wasn't going to hurt her.

"I failed to protect you. It's too late. It's too late," Yuan began to rock back and forth.

"Too late?" Fen glanced at Haun and then Aaron. Her lover's face was strained, and she knew he wanted nothing more than to grab her and take her away from the prisons.

"It's too late, Princess," he said. "They've been called to take you."

Yuan started laughing. He tossed himself back on the bed, rolling slightly in crazy merriment. Fen stumbled back at the sound of it.

"Too late, too late," he kept repeating. "You didn't let me finish my ritual, and now it's too late. I can't protect you from him."

The floor beneath her started to shake. Fen took a quick step back. Her brothers braced their hands against the walls. Yuan stopped laughing but he stayed on the bed, his arms to his sides as he stared at her.

Suddenly, a loud crack sounded. The room shook violently, rafters loosening up above. Yuan screamed as the earth opened up beneath the bed. He was chained to the furniture and as it fell, so did he. His yell was cut short as he hit a jagged piece of newly formed cliff.

The crack started to expand, coming for her.

Fen screamed. Haun jumped back as he was cut off from her, trapped in the room. Shen reached his hand out, yelling at Haun to jump. The oldest brother did, but as he landed next to Shen and Lian, all three of them were cut off by another splintering crack.

Aaron grabbed her from behind as she stood frozen in horror.

"Take her and go," Haun ordered.

Pulling her by the waist, Aaron ran from the room. Fen glanced behind them, screaming as she saw the crack was following her down the hall, as if hungry to suck her down into its depths. It neared her feet. She ran faster. The earth beneath her trembled, opening up. Aaron's hold on her waist kept her from falling as he jerked her up, pushing her ahead of him through the door to the prisons. Her family waited outside, their faces turning to instant shock at the sudden noise, as if they couldn't hear what was happening within the prisons.

Fen tripped again. Aaron grabbed her, flinging her forward at the cost of his own footing. She landed on Jin, who instantly grabbed her.

Looking back, she saw Aaron falling backwards into the crevice. It had stopped moving, but that didn't matter. It was too late.

Fen fought free from Jin's hold to go to him, but she couldn't get to him in time.

"Aaron," she screamed, watching him fall down the impossibly deep cliff into darkness. "No, Aaron!"

Fen was sure her heart stopped beating. She heard commotion behind her, but it didn't register. She made a move to climb down the cliff after him, not thinking of her own safety. He'd given his life to save her when he could've just run away to save himself.

Jin grabbed her arm, pulling her back up. "Fen, no, stop."

"Haun? Shen? Lian?" the empress cried.

"Fen, what happened?" Jin asked.

Her nose burned with the need to cry and her heart physically ached. Pain ripped through her, worse than anything she'd ever felt. Aaron was gone. No one could survive a fall like that.

Her brothers came from within, standing close to the wall as they moved around the cracked earth. Two guards were with them. Their clothes were dusty and Haun's hand was bleeding, but other than that, they looked all right.

"Fen, thank the stars," Shen exclaimed.

"Wait, where's Aaron?" Lian asked.

Fen was racked with a sob, unable to answer as she pointed downward.

"Oh, Fen, no." Lian grabbed his chest. He fell to his knees. Haun reached down and with the help of the guard, pulled him away from the crack in the earth before letting him go. Jin still had a hold on Fen's arm; she tugged, trying to get away.

"Let me go," Fen yelled. "Let me go. You don't understand. He might be alive. I have to go see."

"Fen, I'm sorry." The empress tried to touch her shoulder, but Fen jerked back.

"You didn't want me to have him. Well, you got your wish. Are you happy now, Mother?"

"Fen..." Her mother was pale and shaky as she pulled back.

"I'll go after him," Haun said.

"No," their father commanded. "I won't risk losing my son. I'll go."

Fen looked at her father, about to comment that

he was too old for something like that, when a soft glow encircled his face. She stared in awe.

"Father?" Fen asked. Her awe was repeated by her siblings.

"How?" Shen asked.

"What?" Lian mumbled.

The emperor looked at the crevice, not answering.

Fen turned, realizing suddenly that the light wasn't coming from her father, but reflecting off him. The glow came from inside the crack. A low murmur of voices sounded from deep within.

"*The Ancient...*" Francesca began. "The evil ones are coming up."

"No, wait," Fen said, pointing. "Ancestors."

Faces began to appear in the crevice, forming from the soft glow.

"Grandfather Manchu," Jin said, also pointing. "Guan-yin and..."

"There are so many of them," Francesca whispered.

"Our family," the emperor said.

In the glow, Fen saw a darker movement. Her heart nearly burst as she realized it was Aaron. His dark blue eyes found hers. He looked stunned, but he was alive, carried back to her by her ancestors.

"I thought you could use a little magical assistance of your own," An said from her side.

"Aaron," Fen said, smiling as the pain of his loss was replaced by the joy of his survival. Her body ached as she held out her arms to him. His hand touched hers as ancestors started climbing out of the cliff, smiling happily at them as they walked away from the hole, disappearing as if they'd never been there. The murmur of their voices disappeared with them.

"Well, I'd better be off as well," An said. "We're all going to celebrate, and you know I hate to miss a celebration."

"Wait," the empress said. An turned to her. "Thank you, An, for giving my daughter her heart back."

The spirit nodded but didn't answer as she disappeared.

"Aaron," Fen whispered, as her brothers helped him climb all the way out of the crack. She pulled him to her chest. He grunted in pain.

"Easy," he whispered, lightly holding her with one arm. "They didn't catch me right away."

She eased her hold.

"Are you hurt?" he asked, touching her face.

She shook her head in denial as she looked at him. "Not anymore."

"I hate to break this up, but something is bugging me," Haun said. "Before he died, Yuan said he couldn't protect you from him."

"So?" Shen asked.

"Him, who?" Haun turned to look at Péng You Hall.

"Shing," Fen said. "He was trying to protect me from Shing. It makes sense that they'd be raised the same."

"Guards," Haun ordered. "Arrest Ye Shing."

"Can you walk?" Fen asked Aaron. He nodded. "Good, because I'm going to give that *chusheng xaijiao de xiang huo* a piece of my fist."

The empress gasped at her foul language.

Francesca frowned at Jin, "Did she just say...?"

"Oh, yeah, she just did." Jin nodded.

"*Ooo.*" Francesca shook her head. "Uh, guards, you might want to *rescue* Shing instead, because I think the princess is on the warpath."

Fen marched toward Péng You Hall, livid that Shing could smile to her face, all the time plotting against her.

"Fen, wait," Aaron ordered, limping along behind her.

"Whoa, Aaron, hold on," Shen said. "We need to get you a medic."

"I'll be fine," Aaron protested. "Just stop your sister."

"No thanks, I'd rather take my chances jumping down that crack," Shen answered. "I've never seen her this angry."

"Fen," Haun demanded. "Think about what you're doing."

"Oh, no, I'm done thinking. Shing thinks he can come here and do this. Besides, he can't hurt me. He's out of elements." Fen pushed into the hall, stopping when she realized she didn't know which room was his.

It didn't matter. She saw a door open and Shing poked his head out.

"You," she growled, going for him. "How dare you."

"What?" He tilted his head, smiling innocently at her. "Princess, what is wrong?"

"You tried to kill me," she accused. "And my future husband."

"What?" he gasped in outrage. "I would never."

"The only one you succeeded in hurting was your brother, Yuan. He's dead, Shing. You killed him." Fen felt her family behind her, giving her strength, but they didn't interfere. "It's over, Shing."

"Yuan is dead?" the man gasped. "I don't understand. How can you think I'd kill my own brother?"

Fen kicked at his door in her anger. It didn't open. With a scream of rage, she twisted the latch and slid it open. She went into his room. It was clean, not a thing out of place. A traveling bag was on his bed, latched shut.

"What is all this?" Shing asked. "Emperor, please, what is it you think I've done? What has happened to Yuan? What does the princess mean, he is dead?"

"I don't understand," Fen said, looking around. She went to his bag, riffling through it. The bag was filled with clothes.

"Princess?" Shing said. She glanced back to see the two guards grabbing him to keep him restrained. He tugged to be free, but they held tight.

"You're mad that I didn't choose you, aren't you, Shing?" she demanded. "Tell me, where is it? Where's the altar?"

"Altar?" he repeated.

Her brothers entered the room. Shen and Jin helped her look.

"Fen, nothing's here," Jin said.

"What are you looking for?" Shing demanded. "What is going on here?"

"Where is the altar, Shing?" Fen asked. "Yuan was trying to protect me from you. He didn't want me to marry you. Why, if not to protect me?"

"I don't know what you're talking about," Shing said, his eyes hardening as he raised his voice. "I refuse to listen to this. Where is my brother? What have you done to him? I don't have an altar. I barely pray," he said.

"Fen," Haun called. "Stop. I don't think it's him."

"What do you mean?" Fen asked.

"My father and Yuan are the ones with altars," Shing said. "I don't want anything to do with their religious fanaticism."

"Lord Ye?" Fen gasped.

She saw Haun and Aaron take off down the hall, Aaron a little slower as he limped behind. Fen pushed past Shing, who was still restrained. The nobleman fought to be free. Haun and Aaron pushed into Lord He's room unannounced.

"What?" Lord He screamed. "Get out at once!"

A loud crash sounded. Her mother pulled her arm as she tried to run to see what was happening. Shen, Lian and Jin sprinted past to help. Fen jerked to be free, finally managing to get to the door.

Lian was tapping out fire on the carpet before a long table filled with burning fire pots, knives, basins filled with liquid, and rolled parchments. Lord Ye was dressed in a dark robe, his legs kicking as Haun, Jin and Aaron pinned him down. Aaron yelled in pain as the nobleman kicked him in the ribs. He fell back and Shen was right there to help subdue the man.

Fen tried to go to Aaron but her father grabbed her, holding her back to his chest. Francesca moved to help her husband, but the empress stepped in her way, pushing her back.

"Not with that baby," she ordered.

"You will all rot," Lord Ye yelled. "She is my princess. Mine! I'll kill all who dare to take her."

"Even me?" Shing asked, pushing past them into the room. He stopped, gaping at the altar. His eyes wide, he turned to the man on the floor. "Yuan was trying to protect me. That's why he didn't want me to marry the princess. He knew you'd kill me if I did. That's why he came with us, isn't it? You killed him, didn't you? You killed Yuan."

"He was trying to bind me," Lord Ye growled. "After all I did for that *sishengzi.*"

"How could you?" Shing shook his head. He looked around at the royal family. "I..."

"Shing," his father warned.

"I wash my hands of him," Shing said to the emperor. "He is not my father."

"Shing, I'm sorry," Fen said, feeling horrible for what she'd accused him of being. With the shame she felt pouring out of him, she knew he wasn't involved with Lord Ye's plan. Besides, his own father was plotting to kill him.

Shing opened his mouth but said nothing. He left the room.

"Guards," the emperor ordered. "Arrest Lord Ye for treason, and make sure you chain him completely until we find a way to deal with him. Lord Ye, you are hereby stripped of your title and privilege."

"No," Lord Ye yelled, managing to wriggle free. He crawled toward the altar and grabbed a knife.

"Stop him," Jin yelled, moving to dive after him.

Aaron pushed up from the floor, holding his side.

Lord Ye plunged the knife into his own heart. Everyone stopped moving as he flopped onto the floor.

"Guards, I want it sealed until it can be blessed," the emperor said. "No one goes in or out."

The guards bowed dutifully. The family slowly made their way outside. As they passed, they saw Shing sitting on his bed, his head in his hands.

Fen stopped. Aaron was right beside her. "Shing, I'm sorry I misjudged you."

He looked up, his eyes red as he nodded once, only to let his head drop back down.

"Leave him be," Aaron said quietly. Fen let him lead her away.

31

FEN SAT, watching as the land beneath them flew by in a blur. The *tu di hang* carried them across the prairie of yellow-blue grasses. Aaron was at her side, looking very handsome in the blue and gold tunic he wore. It was the material she'd picked out for him the first night they'd come together, and it looked every bit as good on him as she'd imagined it would. The color really made his dark eyes stand out. His body was healed from the broken ribs and a nearly punctured lung from his fall into the deep crevice, thanks to the palace physician and a few days of bed rest.

After much debate, it was decided by the family to give Lord Ye and his son official noblemen's funerals. Fen felt bad for Shing, as he was ordered to oversee the procession through the village near his home. He was given his father's title of *mingong*, though an uncharacteristically solemn Shing didn't seem to want it. He'd changed drastically since discovering the truth.

Fen still regretted her words and apologized often. He said it was fine, but she didn't believe him. The man was grieving and had no family. She could think of nothing worse. The emperor sent Shen and Lian home with Shing to search the family estate for clues as to other practitioners of *The Ancient Way*. They had yet to return.

An and the empress stayed true to their words and called a truce, though An grumbled to Fen that the empress watered down her offering. Fen refused to get into the middle of it.

Francesca and Jin spent a week at the palace. The empress, obviously swayed to like her foreign-born daughter-by-marriage since she was carrying a grandchild, did her best to make peace with the woman. It was all Francesca could do to put up with the overabundance of motherly attention, or so she'd claimed when Fen was alone with her. But, Fen could tell there was a part of her that liked the atten-tion. Francesca never knew her own mother, and the empress was the closest thing she'd ever have to one.

"What are you thinking about?" Aaron asked.

Fen saw her brother Haun was on the other side of the ship. The three of them sailed alone, on their way to visit with Lady Hsin. Sighing, she reached to hold his hand. "I'm thinking about how things worked out and how lucky I am to have you."

"Not everything has worked out," he said, looking into the distance. "There is still Lady Hsin."

"I told you, Aaron, I know the woman. She's not cruel. I'm sure she'll see reason. Besides, who wouldn't want me in their family?"

He laughed. "But if she does refuse me..."

Fen could feel his pain, as real as if it were her own. She knew he was worried. The old rejection ran deep inside him. Smiling, she patted his arm. "If she does, then she is a fool. You're my husband, Prince Aaron. You don't need her. You have a family. You have me, and I love you."

He smiled. Their wedding had been fast, performed the day after Lord Ye's death. In fact, it was so fast that they had skipped the bridal procession in the sedan and the ceremonial clothes, which caused Francesca to grumble since she'd been forced to endure the hideous platform shoes of tradition when she was tricked into marrying Jin.

The couple had even skipped waiting for the astrologers' blessing on the union. She loved Aaron, and she was going to spend her life with him, no matter anyone else's opinion on the matter. However, the astrologers did get their say, as they barely had time to run in and claim that they approved of the match before it was done. Fen had laughed because she didn't need their approval. The women didn't care. They had their place in the history scrolls when it came to Fen's wedding.

They were married inside the Exalted Hall in the presence of the royal family—all but Princess Mei. None of them had heard from Mei, but the youngest Zhang was in Fen's thoughts. They paid homage to the earth and sky and to their ancestors. They left a jug of wine at the altar. Fen saw An sneaking in to grab it as they were walking out. Aaron had been sore, so she took him straight to bed, skipping the party. It was decided that a celebration would be held after they got back from Lady Hsin's.

And though the empress wasn't thrilled by Fen's defiance, she'd accepted Aaron into the family.

The village of *Haohe* came into sight. It was nestled in the valley under Lady Hsin's sprawling mansion home, which sat higher on a hill. Fen could see the mansion as they entered on the opposite side of town. Winding roads led up the hill, breaking off to lead to several buildings that housed Lady Hsin's factories and warehouses. Long fields of mulberries grew along the side of the hill, as it plateaued onto a more even ground to the side. The field disappeared around the hill. Fen could see several workers hovering above the plants as they tended the crops with long metal arms that reached out from the bottom of their harvesters. The village itself was a maze of short, thatched-roof farmhouses.

Haun steered the craft along the outskirts of town, going around it along a higher ridge that would lead to Lady Hsin's. Villagers came out to watch them, pointing as the *tu di hang* passed by. It wasn't a spectacular thing to see the royal family visit Lady Hsin's. The villagers were well used to noble and royal guests.

"Piers Aaron, I swear," Fen heard someone shout. She saw a man pointing up at them, frantically waving his hand.

"Everyone knows everyone here," Aaron said, his voice tight.

Fen smiled, grabbed his face and kissed him soundly for all to see. When she pulled back, his eyes had lightened some and he was smiling tenderly at her. "Let them gossip about you now."

He gave a small laugh, touching her face. "I'm still waiting to wake up from this. It feels like a dream. No man could ever deserve to be so lucky as to have you, my sweet princess."

"If you do wake up, make sure you come and find me. I'll be waiting." She winked, moving to wave at some nearby children, who tried to run to keep up with the land craft. They didn't make it very far. She lightly touched the small embroidered circle on his chest. It was the royal dragon emblazoned on his tunic, marking him as a Zhang prince. "It is I who am lucky to have you, my sweet rock."

"Rock?" he laughed.

"Mmm, butterflies need rocks." She winked, reminding him of more intimate times.

He instantly moaned, glancing over her body. "That's not fair. You know we can't do anything right now."

"I know." She grinned. "Mmm, but I was just thinking of how good your hands felt on my body. Like last night, when you had me on my hands and knees and—"

Aaron put his hand over her mouth to stop her. His breathing had deepened, and she could feel he was aroused. She'd meant to tease him but found she'd also teased herself. Her body was awakened with the memory, and she desperately wanted to find a place to run and hide so they could finish what she'd started.

"There are many rooms we still need to make love in at the palace," he said, grinning. It was her turn to moan. They'd already sneaked out to the imperial gardens to have a fast romp by the small, hidden waterfall. Every other time they barely made it to the bed, let alone out of the royal chambers where he now lived with her.

"Ugh, okay," she moaned, "I give. No more until we can do something about it."

"Agreed." His tone dropped, and his voice had gotten very husky.

Fen felt the land craft shift and looked up. They were making their way up the winding road to Lady Hsin's. The mansion was long with a tiled roof much like that on the palace, only it was brown. An extended terrace crossed over the paved front side of the house, leading to three different doors. The largest door in the middle led to the main portion of the house; the other two near the sides were guest suites. Fen often stayed in the suites.

She wasn't surprised to see Lady Hsin come personally from the front of the house to greet her. The woman's smile faded as Haun drew the land craft to a halt before her door. Her eyes stared up at Aaron.

Fen watched, seeing how he looked down and away, as if an automatic gesture.

She touched his hand and smiled. He looked at her, seeming to draw strength from her nearness. Haun went to the side of the craft and ran his hand over the eye to lower the stairs. He was the first one down, moving to raise his hand to his sister. Fen followed him, smiling at Lady Hsin.

The woman was just as she remembered, elegant in long, flowing green silk robes. They didn't form to her body but fluttered around her in the breeze. Thinner strips of material caught up, blowing to the side. Her gray and black hair was pulled up, gathered into a bun at the top of her head. Fine wrinkles lined her eyes, but they only added a sense of command to her rather than age.

"Princess, you travel much lighter than usual," Lady Hsin said, noting her lack of guards.

"Married women are given more lenience," Fen answered, smiling innocently at her.

"Married?" Lady Hsin glanced at Aaron.

Fen didn't see any point in delaying the reason why they'd come. She didn't want to put Aaron through that. If the woman chose to be difficult, they'd just leave.

"*Shi.*" Fen motioned toward Aaron. "You know my husband, Prince Aaron."

"Prince?" the woman repeated. Her face was white as she looked at Aaron. She put her hand over her heart, shaking her head as she looked at him. "Prince. No one deserves it more."

Aaron frowned at her words, and Fen knew he didn't trust the woman. She couldn't blame him.

"I longed for the day you would find a way past my harsh words. I'd hoped, beyond everything, that if I educated you and gave you a chance to meet noble-women, that you would find a way to win their heart. I never imagined that you would win yourself a princess."

She was shaking as she walked toward her grand-son, holding out her hand. Aaron looked at it, not taking it.

"How I've prayed to have my words back. You were so little, looked so much like my Genji except for your father's eyes. Randall was such a reckless, free-spirited man. I suppose that is why your mother loved him. I was so sad to have lost her that I lost my temper as well. I've regretted it ever since but knew if you were to be the fine man I see today, you would have to work hard. I gave you every chance I could, and look at you…"

Aaron looked at her hand and then at her. "You never said before. Why do you say so now?"

"Why get your hopes up when I couldn't take back what was done?" Lady Hsin's hand fell. "I understand that you don't trust me. You think I only say this now because you are a prince."

"Don't you?" he asked.

"It is because you are now a prince that I *can* say it. I can never hope that you'll forgive me, but I hope you know that I did try to make it right by you. I gave you run of all that I have when I could not give you my name."

"That's why we've come," Fen said. She looked at Haun. He pulled a parchment from his robes and handed it to Lady Hsin. "It gives you right by imperial decree to reinstate Aaron as your grandson, undoing what was done."

"But," Lady Hsin didn't open it, "that's never been granted. Such a statement can't be undone."

"He is the emperor," Haun said. "He can do anything."

"Do you change your mind now?" Aaron asked, his tone hard.

"Is this the only reason you came to tell me? Do

you need me to sign in order to remain together?" Lady Hsin looked at Fen.

"No, we don't," Fen said. "Your blessing is not required."

"Oh." She unrolled the parchment and looked at it. Reaching for her hair, she pushed at the bun until she withdrew a small writing wand from it. Without another word, she signed it and gave it back to Haun. He rolled it and stuck it in his robes once more. "I am happy to have you back in the family, Aaron. Maybe someday, you can see clear to forgiving an old woman."

Lady Hsin nodded and turned to go inside her home. Fen looked at Aaron. He sighed, stepping hesitantly after her.

"We don't need your blessing," Aaron said softly, "but I would like it."

Lady Hsin stopped, her head falling forward. Slowly, she turned, tears in her eyes. She nodded, holding out her hands for a hug. Aaron went forward and hugged her. Fen felt his joy wash over her and was happy for him. Now his family was complete.

When he pulled away, Lady Hsin demanded he come inside with her. Fen went to her husband, threading her arm through his as they walked.

"I can't tell you how proud I am of you. All those

designs you created..." Lady Hsin started talking, going on nonstop like she'd been bottling everything she wanted to say to him for years.

Fen looked up at him and whispered, "It looks like that alone time might be put off for a while."

He grinned, and she felt his happiness inside her, making her own complete. "Now everything has worked out for the best."

"I love you," she mouthed, not interrupting Lady Hsin's ongoing praise of her grandson.

"And I you, my tempting little butterfly."

The End

New York Times & *USA TODAY* Bestselling Author

Michelle loves to travel and try new things, whether it's a paranormal investigation of an old Vaudeville Theatre or climbing Mayan temples in Belize. She believes life is an adventure fueled by copious amounts of coffee.

Newly relocated to the American South, Michelle is involved in various film and documentary projects with her talented director husband. She is mom to a fantastic artist. And she's managed by a dog and cat who make sure she's meeting her deadlines.

For the most part she can be found wearing pajama pants and working in her office. There may or may not be dancing. It's all part of the creative process.

Come say hello! Michelle loves talking with readers on social media!

www.MichellePillow.com

facebook.com/AuthorMichellePillow

twitter.com/michellepillow

instagram.com/michellempillow

bookbub.com/authors/michelle-m-pillow

goodreads.com/Michelle_Pillow

amazon.com/author/michellepillow

youtube.com/michellepillow

pinterest.com/michellepillow

COMPLIMENTARY EXCERPTS

TRY BEFORE YOU BUY!

GALAXY ALIEN MAIL ORDER BRIDES

The Series:
Spark
Flame
Blaze
Ice
Frost
Snow

Blaze

Sev (aka Blaze) isn't looking for commitment, but there is no way in hell he's letting his brother go to Earth to search for a woman by himself. He's prepared to yank the idiot out of every jail house and ice cream parlor (don't ask) if he has to. It wouldn't be the first time. He can handle a good fight. But what this alpha isn't prepared for was the hardheaded beauty determined to follow him home.

Prologue Excerpt

Summer Setting Celebration
Frxsolis Settlement, Planet Bravon, Solarus <u>Q</u>uadrant

Sevglarkenbauer watched through the haze of liquor as couples paired up to dance. The old music was the same set of songs he heard every year, and he found comfort in knowing the lyrics before they were sang. There were only a few single women in the settlement, and he had no desire to ask any of them to dance. Instead, he sat with the other ash miners, drinking the stout Killian liquor, and pushing himself into the mind-numbing oblivion that so much alcohol would inevitably bring.

Buried completely underground, the mining settlement of Frxsolis was made up of clusters of decommissioned spaceships and hollowed tunnels. Solar energy powered the entire settlement. Rows of artificial lights lined the metal rectangle of the commons room where they now celebrated the end of the intense summer season. Long ago, before Bravon's fiery surface had buried the ship's hull beneath a layer of lava and rock, it had been a sky worthy transport vessel. Now, forever entombed beneath the ground, it was the common area of the settlement—a place where they gathered to dine and sometimes, like tonight, for drinking and dancing. As the mining tunnels expanded, they sometimes ran across the ships, which suggested the planet had once been an alien dumping ground for space wreckage. Those were interesting salvage finds.

During the cooler hours, which were still inhabitable on the surface, extendable turbines harnessed the power of the nearby suns to sustain life below by refueling the solar generators. Nearly three thousand Killians lived in Frxsolis. They were a proud, hardworking people. A person had to be to survive in such a harsh environment. Ships had to have special protectant coat even to land on Bravon. For this reason, the only visitors they received were ash haulers. It made the dating pool very, very small.

Sev had gone out several times to maintenance the turbines. Even if he could survive long term on the surface without a protective suit, he wouldn't want to. The suns never set on Bravon, but the light did lessen into a brilliant display of white streaks across the purple and blue heavens. The slick ash sand made it hard to walk, and the desolate charcoal landscape was only broken up by the lava that oozed over the side of the mountain in a fiery waterfall. The bulk of the molten stream sludged into a nearby river, nearly stagnant as it bubbled, sending hot sprays of orange into the air. No living thing survived on the surface, so the only sound was the small clinking noises made by the lava pebbles as they cooled on their way to the ground from the top of the waterfall.

Sev realized he was staring at the ceiling and turned his eyes back to the couples. He took another drink, only to find his cup was empty. He lowered it back to his lap, too drunk to move from his chair. More than likely, he would sleep right where he was.

Ash mining was a hard existence, but they were Killians and Killians never shied away from a challenge. The artificial lights led out of the commons into the maze of tunnels that created the underground settlement's pathways. Several of the corridors still had torches. They weren't really for light so much as a warning system. Sev looked at the fire often. If the flames began to flicker rapidly, it was possible the settlement had been breached, just as it had been the night his parents died when an air lock malfunctioned in the mines. Heat from outside flooded a shaft along the outskirts.

Why was he thinking of that? It had happened so long ago.

He blinked drunkenly, trying to focus his vision on his nearby brother. Vinglarkenbauer yelled more than sang the lyrics of the old song, not bothering to stay on note as his voice joined the others around him. Sev gave a small laugh. Vin was younger than him by several years, and, even though he was now a man, he was still Sev's responsibility.

Sev adjusted is legs and again tried to drink from the empty cup. He grumbled under his breath, this time setting the cup on the table next to him. A figure danced before his view, swaying back and forth. Sev scowled, leaning to look past his cousin, Kalglarkenbauer. Kal danced back in front of his vision and, just as Sev was going to push the annoyance out of the way, Kal handed him another cup filled with solar water to replace the drink he'd just finished.

This gesture automatically changed Sev's drunken annoyance into a welcoming wave. He grinned. "Where have you been? Please tell me Grentakinkensauer didn't trap you in the south tunnels again and try to give you the pointy thumb. Tell me, did she mark you as her own."

Kal shivered dramatically. "I wouldn't dare dream of seducing her away from you."

"She's all yours, cousin," Sev answered. "I want no piece of that crazy."

"Don't you wish we could meet some women who we haven't known since childhood?" Kal sighed wistfully. "It has been too many years since we took extended joint time off from the ash mines, and even longer since we've left the planet. Don't you think it's about time we went somewhere?"

Sev shrugged. Sure, a little female companionship would be a welcome change. "You want to go to the Larceny Casino again? Is Vin even allowed back onboard after last time?"

"I'm not sure. I'd have to check. But I was thinking something a little different." Kal smiled and tapped the device he held close to his chest.

"What do you have there?" Sev nodded to the device as he took a long drink. Sweet slumber was close. "A signature pad? What are you doing with a signature pad?"

"Hey, is that Grenta?" Kal asked. "It looks like she's coming to ask you for a dance."

Sev pushed up in his seat to look around. He felt a tug at his hand and glanced down to see Kal holding his thumb. The sudden change in position caused his head to swirl and his vision to darken. Just as he was about to ask his cousin what he thought he was doing holding his hand, he felt the blessed numbness of alcohol taking him.

"Don't you worry, Sev. You're going to thank me for this later." Kal's words barely registered as darkness flooded his mind.

MichellePillow.com

LOVE POTIONS

BY MICHELLE M. PILLOW

Warlocks MacGregor Book 1
Contemporary Paranormal Scottish Warlocks

A little magickal mischief never hurt anyone...

Erik MacGregor, from a clan of ancient Scottish warlocks, isn't looking for love. After centuries, it's not even a consideration...until he moves in next door to Lydia Barratt. It's clear that the shy beauty wants nothing to do with him, but he's drawn to her nonetheless and determined to win her over.

Lydia Barratt just wants to be left alone to grow flowers and make lotions in her old Victorian house. The last thing she needs is a demanding Scottish man meddling in her private life. Just because he's gorgeous and totally rocks a kilt doesn't mean she's going to fall for his seductive manner.

But Erik won't give up and just as Lydia let's her guard down, his sister decides to get involved. Her little love potion prank goes terribly wrong, making Lydia the target of his sudden embarrassingly obsessive behavior. They'll have to find a way to pull Erik out of the spell fast when it becomes clear that Lydia has more than a lovesick warlock to worry about. Evil lurks within the shadows and it plans to use Lydia, alive or dead, to take out Erik and his clan for good.

Love Potions Excerpt

"Ly-di-ah! I sit beneath your window, laaaass, singing 'cause I loooove your a—"

"For the love of St. Francis of Assisi, someone call a vet. There is an injured animal screaming in pain outside," Charlotte interrupted the flow of music in ill-humor.

Lydia lifted her forehead from the kitchen table. Her windows and doors were all locked, and yet Erik's endlessly verbose singing penetrated the barrier of glass and wood with ease.

Charlotte held her head and blinked heavily. Her red-rimmed eyes were filled with the all too poignant look of a hangover. She took a seat at the table and laid her head down. Her moan sounded something like, "I'm never moving again."

"You need fluids," Lydia prescribed, getting up to pour unsweetened herbal tea from the pitcher in the fridge. She'd mixed it especially for her friend. It was Gramma Annabelle's hangover recipe of willow bark, peppermint, carrot, and ginger. The old lady always had a fresh supply of it in the house while she was alive. Apparently, being a natural witch also meant in partaking in natural liquors. Annabelle had kept a steady supply of moonshine stashed in the basement. If the concert didn't stop soon she might try to find an old bottle.

"*Ly-di-ah!*"

"Omigod. Kill me," Charlotte moaned. "No. Kill him. Then kill me."

"*Ly-di-ah!*"

Erik had been singing for over an hour. At first, he'd tried to come inside. She'd not invited him and the barrier spell sent him sprawling back into the yard. He didn't seem to mind as he found a seat on some landscaping timbers and began his serenade. The last time she'd asked him to be quiet, he'd gotten louder and overly enthusiastic. In fact, she'd been too scared to pull back the curtains for a clearer look, but she was pretty sure he'd been dancing on her lawn, shaking his kilt.

"Omigod," Charlotte muttered, pushing up and angrily going to a window. Then grimacing, she said, "Is he wearing a tux jacket with his kilt?"

"Don't let him see you," Lydia cried out in a panic. It was too late. The song began with renewed force.

"He's..." Charlotte frowned. "I think it's dancing."

Since the damage was done, Lydia joined Charlotte at the window. Erik grinned. He lifted his arms to the side and kicked his legs, bouncing around the yard like a kid on too much sugar. "Maybe it's a traditional Scottish dance?"

Both women tilted their heads in unison as his kilt kicked up to show his perfectly formed ass.

"He's not wearing..." Charlotte began.

"I know. He doesn't," Lydia answered. Damn, the man had a fine body. Too bad Malina's trick had turned him insane.

www.MichellePillow.com